HOUR OF RECKONING

A shower of stinging sand dashed against his cheek. The whine of the bullet followed and then the heavy, clanging report of the rifle. He looked up, for the sound had come from the lip of the rocks far above him. At the same time, a shout of triumph roared up from the men of Grenacho who were waiting below.

He understood then, angrily. They had simply tricked him. One or two of the party had circled to the left and climbed the height. From that safe position they could shoot him down at their leisure.

He looked up and saw the wink of the sun on a rifle barrel. He snatched up his own weapon and fired. There was an instant's pause, then a heavy impact knocked him breathless. A rifle ball had crunched through his shoulder.

The weirdly pitched yell from the rocks informed Grenacho's men that their enemy had been hit!

Warner Books by
MAX BRAND

Man from Savage Creek

Trouble Trail

Timbal Gulch Trail

The Sheriff Rides

Valley Vultures

Marbleface

The Return of the Rancher

Bull Hunter

Wild Freedom

Mountain Riders

Slow Joe

Happy Jack

Happy Valley

Max Brand's Best Western
  Stories

The King Bird Rides

The Long Chance

Mistral

Smiling Charlie

The Rancher's Revenge

The Dude

Silvertip's Roundup

The Man from the Wilderness

Gunfighter's Return

Rider of the High Hill

Way of the Lawless

Storm on the Range

Thunder Moon's Challenge

Thunder Moon Strikes

Gunman's Gold

The Making of a Gunman

Lawless Land

THE TRAIL TO SAN TRISTE

Max Brand

WARNER BOOKS

A Warner Communications Company

WARNER BOOKS EDITION

Originally published in 1924 in *Western Story Magazine* as *Four without Fear*, written under the name of George Owen Baxter.

This Warner Books Edition is published by arrangement with Dodd, Mead & Company

Warner Books, Inc.
666 Fifth Avenue
New York, N.Y. 10103

 A Warner Communications Company

Printed in the United States of America

First Warner Books Printing: February, 1985

10 9 8 7 6 5 4 3 2 1

1

Three detectives met in the lobby of the Paso del Norte in El Paso town. Only Thomas was of El Paso; the others were Ingram, from San Francisco, and Walker, from Denver. They knew each other from the old days, when they had learned to follow a trail and handle a gun.

They greeted one another without surprise, for El Paso is one of those crossings of the ways where people from every corner of the globe will turn up. It is the northern gate to Mexico to which many come to peer through, as it were, into the mystery and the strangeness of old Mexico, while a few make up their packs and start on the long journey for wealth or for unknown adventure.

"What's what?" asked Ingram of San Francisco.

"I'm doing a little stunt in this town," said Thomas of El Paso. "Just now, I'm keeping an eye on the hardest nut west of the Mississippi; he's here in the hotel at present."

"He may be the hardest but one," said Ingram. "But the youngster I followed down here from 'Frisco is the prizewinner."

"What's on him?"

"Nothing, except what I can hang."

"Boys," said Walker of Denver, "don't be chesty about the crooks you're chasing. I'm after a fellow who's been everything from a strikebreaker to a smuggler and a thief. H. K. Halsey is the meat I've staked out!"

There was a murmur of awed admiration from the others.

"Where is he now?"

"Right here in the hotel; just went up to room 1122, as a matter of fact."

"Why," cried Thomas, "my man has gone to the same room!"

"Who is he?"

"Si Denny."

"My man, Marmont, went to that floor," broke in Ingram. "I didn't get the room number, but he must have gone to the same place. What's in that room?"

"A queer-looking sap named Joseph Simon," answered Thomas. "I thought he was crooked when I first saw him. Now I know it! I'll lay ten to one that the four of 'em are cooking up a deal that will make your hair stand on end."

"Marmont, Denny, and Halsey!" said Ingram softly. "All working together at one job. What the devil can be in the wind?"

"Mix those three together in equal parts and touch them off with a chance to work, and they'll blow a hole to China," commented Walker. "I'd give a good deal to know what they're doing at this minute!"

He would have been infinitely surprised, however, if he could have looked into the room, for the three fugitives were seated in a semicircle gazing at an oil painting with a profound and silent interest. If these were criminals, there was nothing about them to indicate it.

Halsey, the central figure of the trio, was the eldest, being perhaps fifty. He had a flushed, pouchy, rather dissipated look, with rather bulging, pale-blue eyes. He looked like a harmless fellow who was a bit too fond of rich living; and the limp with which he walked would have been taken, ordinarily, for a touch of the gout instead of old bullet wounds.

His right-hand neighbor, Silas Denny, was a long-drawn-out New Englander, with huge hands and feet and a big head, worthy of a philosopher, balanced uneasily upon the end of a scrawny neck which seemed to be hinged exactly in the middle behind the Adam's apple. He had the leathery brown skin of a sailor, quiet gray eyes surrounded with wrinkles of observation, and a voice both tremendously low and marvelously rough. Its vibration seemed to make a whole room quiver.

The third man was Pierre Gaston Marmont. He was quite unlike the others, being small in body, not past his twenty-fourth year at the most, nervously quick in all his movements, with the pale, worn face of one nervously exhausted. An ordinary life killed him with ennui; he could not exist without the stimulus of great excitement.

The three continued to stare for some time at the picture, which was that of a young man of indeterminate age—perhaps between twenty-five and thirty. The painting was full-length, and showed him standing easily with a hand upon one hip and his face turned in three-quarter view.

"Closely and more closely, my friends," urged Joseph Simon from the back of the room. "I have photographs of the picture, but phographs will not give the color of the eyes, the sallow complexion, the gloss of the black hair."

He hurried forward and, placing himself to one side of the picture, began to point out its characteristics like a teacher before a class.

"Consider, my friends," said he, "the grace and the elegant slimness of these hands, with the faint network of blue veins mottling them. That is how close I wish to have you look at this picture. I want you to print the details in your minds. I want you to absorb it."

He grew fired with his enthusiasm; a spot of color glowed in the center of each pale cheek; his humped back straightened a little; he swept the long, silvery hair back from his forehead.

"Consider the body of the man. Tear off the clothes with your imaginations. Be anatomists. Discover the small bones, the long, smooth muscles—a body made for speed and lightness. Such a man could leap inches above his own height, run like a greyhound, and strike like a prizefighter.

"There is the face, finally and above all. You see the thin, straight nose; the narrow eyebrows, well arched; the long, narrow jaw, lean and hard like the jaw of a bull terrier—a fighting jaw, my dear friends—the thin lips, quite colorless; the lofty forehead, and the black hair. You observe these things; you write down the details in your brains!"

He turned to them with a singular, imploring gesture, his hands palm up, his eyes wistful, his shoulders shrugged.

He went on: "This man is intelligent, but lazy minded. He

gambles not to win, but for the excitement of losing. He is constantly in trouble with others. He is rude and imperious with his equals. He is astonishingly gentle and condescending with his inferiors—with his servants, let us say."

"Enough, enough, enough!" said Marmont, rapidly and nervously. "I see his mind more clearly than his body. What more?"

"That is it—the mind is all important. With such a brain, the differences in face and body can be endured. They will not matter."

"What's the name of the chap in the picture?" asked Halsey.

"He has no name."

"Eh?"

The three looked at one another, a little bewildered.

"He has no name," continued Simon. "He is created by the hand of man, not by God. He is not one man; he is a whole race!"

There was no answer. They kept their exclamations to themselves.

"Now, sirs," went on Joseph Simon, "we come back to business. Your first task is, you will say, very easy. You are simply to go wandering. Your traveling expenses will be paid. Your pay continues the same—for every week of your work— two hundred dollars. In short, I ask you to enjoy a lazy vacation—using your eyes only. Do you understand?"

"Well?" asked Denny in his immense, deep voice.

"You are to use your eyes only—and find for me a man who is of this type."

"That's a queer face," said Denny. "Might go around the world without seeing it."

"I cannot ask for the impossible," said Simon. "I only ask for the type—the type—the type! Is not that clear? You will find the type. He must be not less than five feet and eleven inches in height—perhaps an inch or so taller. He must be not less than twenty-two years in age or more than twenty-five. He must be clever, reckless, cool-headed. He must, certainly, speak Spanish like a native.

"I ask for a great deal you see. But I have secured the

three sharpest pairs of eyes in the world to help me. You will begin, sirs? You will begin today?''

They observed him with thoughtful eyes; each was hunting through his memory; each was recalling some face or faces which might serve for the purpose.

''There is a bonus to him who finds the man,'' said Simon. ''There is a bonus to him who finds the man and brings him to El Paso. That bonus is five thousand dollars—after I have talked with him and been satisfied!''

''Well,'' said Denny, ''does our job end when we land him?''

''No, no! That is only the beginning. When he is secured, then we are ready to embark on the great adventure.''

He sank into a chair and buried his face in his hands, trembling with emotion and exhaustion. The others glanced at him with a suggestion of contempt in their eyes. Then they said farewell, one by one, and left the room.

2

Fired by the talk of Joseph Simon, armed with their memories of the painting and with photographic copies of it in their pockets, the three separated and each went his way. Off to San Francisco sped Pierre Marmont to find again one whom he remembered as resembling that face in the painting.

To St. Louis fled Hubert Halsey as fast as express trains could whirl him along. But Silas Denny merely hired a buggy and started out on a leisurely journey along the bank of the Rio Grande. When he came to a village, he made a halt; he took walks through the streets; and in the eating rooms where he took his meals, he was careful to bring the photograph from his pocket and display it on the table.

Every one who saw it lingered to take another glance. It was such a speaking picture that people were continually trying to recognize it. In six days he made a half dozen futile trips to run down the chance clues which came his way, but he found nothing, saving in one case a man whose face indeed was strikingly like that of the painting, but the fellow was at least thirty, spoke a corrupted Spanish slang, rather than the pure Castilian, and apparently was not blessed with brains.

But still Denny refused to go to a great city where he would have an opportunity of seeing a hundred times as many faces daily as he could in this careless rambling through little towns or empty desert roads. For he said to himself that only luck could bring him to what he wanted, and he might have luck at a crossroads village as well as in a metropolis. He was a great believer in predestined fate, was Denny.

So he continued for ten days, and on the tenth day he was ready to surrender his task; it had been too perfectly fruitless. He stopped that evening in a little dusty village not far from the border, a town where the Mexicans were to the Americans as five to one, a sleepy, cheerless town of whitewashed dobe huts.

A small sandstorm had caught Denny on his way that afternoon, and when he reached the hotel he went to a room and undressed, shook out the sand from his clothes as well as he could, took a sponge bath, and then went down to his supper. He was late, and the meal was cold, consisting of half-fried bacon and soggy boiled potatoes with coffee both bitter and weak.

Such wretched food was not calculated to improve the disposition of the traveler; and as he studied the photograph which, as usual, he had put beside his plate, he was tempted to tear it up and send word to Joseph Simon that he could go to the devil and take this ungrateful job with him.

A red-necked cowpuncher who sat at the little table just in front of Denny, having finished his meal, rose in haste and started to leave the room, but as he reached the side of Denny he paused with a sudden jingling of his spurs and studied the picture. A great sun-reddened hand was rested on the edge of

Denny's table, and now a voice which matched the hand made query: "Might you be a friend of the Kid?"

Denny looked up into a glowering face.

"I might be," he said coldly. "Are you?"

"I ain't!" said the other with great decision. "Which if you aim to see him, you might take him a message from me!"

There could not have been a more inappropriate time for such a greeting to Silas Denny. The long, striking muscles of his arms gathered and bunched in hard knots and moving ripples. He said with misleading pleasantness: "I got my start running errands, son, but I've quit that job."

The big cowpuncher turned purple, and his throat swelled with his passion. He, too, had faced that sandstorm, and the grit was itching and chafing his body at that very moment.

"Stranger," he said hotly, "I got an idea that I might give you something to take along to the Kid that you wouldn't have to talk about; it might talk for itself!"

With that he balled his great fist. Si Denny had grown as pale as the other was red, and he had become extremely thoughtful.

"Suppose we go outside where we'll have room to talk," said he. "A little room like this sort of cramps my voice."

The cowpuncher agreed with savage energy, and they departed to the broad, noisy street, where a tangle of children were playing.

"Are you ready?" said the cowpuncher.

"Waiting!" said Denny.

He dodged a pile-driver punch, slipping under the shooting arm, and dipped his fist into the ribs of the cowman. The latter sat suddenly down in the dust and wrapped his arms about his body. But Denny went thoughtfully back into the hotel, shaking his head and damning himself silently.

For he felt that he had thrown away the only good clue which he had, as yet, come across. Yonder fellow who still sat in the dust of the street, rocking back and forth and gasping for breath, evidently thought he knew the subject of the photograph. He had even given it a name.

It was rather an uncanny thing. It made Si Denny feel as

though the picture itself had been embodied, though first created out of the imagination of a painter. The whole affair was a little mysterious to Si. He hardly dared to ask himself questions about it. Why the picture was painted at such a great price; why, if it represented no living man, Joseph Simon was so anxious to find a man who closely resembled it; what purpose would be attempted after a likeness to the painting were discovered in flesh and blood, if that were possible—these queries he shut into the back of his brain. For he hated weird and unearthly things.

He was a practical man, was Si Denny. He believed that there was nothing in the world which could not be computed, unit by unit. For the abstractions he felt only disgust. Since he felt very few emotions himself, he believed that other people who talked of friendship between man and man and love between man and woman were hypocrites.

As for friends, he had none and he wanted none; the secret of his success was the lone hand which he played. He attempted nothing which he could not complete in every detail unassisted. Accordingly, he had reached the age of forty without serving a prison term, though his criminal record stretched over a period of twenty-two years. He was surrounded with a thick mist of suspicion, but no detective of the many who had trailed him had ever been able to look through the mist and state exactly what he had done.

He had reached the age of forty, then, without ever failing and without ever having a human being to rejoice with him in his nefarious successes. He gained his only social pleasure by observing the follies and the weaknesses and the absurdities of the human race.

Being such a man as he was, he despised all emotional displays, and above all he detested any exhibition of anger. The result was that he was more highly mortified at having given way to his temper than he was pleased by having beaten the cowpuncher. The instant's satisfaction of driving his hard fist into the body of the latter in no way compensated him for his shame in having found it necessary to fight. Above all, that mortification might have a meaning in hard terms of dollars and cents, for yonder was a man who might have led him indirectly to his goal.

Going back into the hotel, therefore, he sat down in the shabby little lobby near an elderly man whose careless dress and immense sombrero and shop-made boots proclaimed him a cattleman.

"Who," asked Si Denny, "is the Kid?"

"What kid?" asked the other sharply.

"*The* Kid," responded Denny, hoping against hope.

But the other regarded him for a moment under bent brows.

"Are you a stranger to these parts?" he asked.

"I am," said Denny.

"Well, then, my friend, you take my advice and keep strange. If you heard about the Kid, don't ask no more questions."

"Why not?"

"He ain't good luck—that's all!"

With this, as though to put an end to a conversation which was not to his taste, the cowman rose from his chair and walked to another part of the room.

Si Denny rose likewise. He was growing more and more convinced that a great discovery was just around the corner from him, if he could only learn in what way to start toward it.

He went to the proprietor. That fat, amiable gentleman sat with his shirt sleeves rolled up to his plump elbows, oozing perspiration at every pore, and smiling upon the world.

"Do you," asked Si Denny, "know the Kid?"

The smile was stricken from the face of the proprietor. He looked suddenly about him, and seemed relieved that no one was in hearing distance.

"I thought you was a stranger here," he said coldly. "Doggone me if I thought that you knowed the Kid!"

"I'm askin' you about him," said Si Denny.

"This ain't my day for talking, nor my night neither," answered the other with the greatest resolution. "The Kid is the Kid. His business ain't my business, and my business ain't the Kid's business. I let it go at that, and I ask you to let it go at that. Hello, Charlie, I got some news for you!"

With this he waved to a man who had just entered the room, and Denny was unable to stand in his place in the face of this inescapable hint. He turned slowly away, therefore, and lingered for a time in the deepest thought. He could see the proprietor and Charlie talking softly and swiftly together, and their eyes were fixed upon him. Very evidently his query had made him the subject of the conversation.

Back to the street went Si Denny.

"You got a sheriff in this here town?" he asked the first man he met.

He had to repeat the question in Spanish, and then the other pointed out a dobe building something larger than the other houses and named it as the residence of the sheriff. He believed that the officer of the law was now in town.

To the door of the sheriff's house went Si Denny, slowly, full of thought. The wind had died down, but still the air was thick with the finest, unsettled desert dust, and above the dust the stars looked dimly down. He tapped at the door of the sheriff's house and that worthy came instantly to speak to him. "Might you be the sheriff?" asked Denny.

The sheriff nodded and stepped outside.

He was a big, lean, well-built man, a man of action by his step, his eye, his crisp voice. Si Denny, weighing him, found him all man.

"Anything wrong?" asked the sheriff.

"I'm just looking for information."

"Fire away, partner. I'll tell you mostly anything I know. Except the price of tequila!" He chuckled at that.

"All I want to do," said Denny, "isn't worth the price of a drink. I just want to find out about the Kid!"

The sheriff whirled upon him with a frown. "Who told you to come ask me that?" he said hoarsely.

"What's wrong?"

A flood of oaths broke from the stern lips of the man of the law.

"I'll slam a few of 'em in jail—these gents that got such a funny sense of humor. I'll show 'em what's what with me," roared the sheriff. "That's been made enough of a joke of. What's more—I'll start right in by locking *you* up!"

"What's wrong with me? What have I done?" asked Si Denny, considerably amazed.

"Breaking the peace," said the sheriff. "Trying to make a riot here in this town. It can't be done. By the heavens, I'll show you who's the master here. I'll show you who stands for law and order!"

Si Denny retreated in haste, with apologies.

"Who sent you?" bellowed the sheriff as Si went off.

"The fellow who runs the hotel," said Denny, unable to resist this bit of malice.

"Darn his fat soul! I'll fry him thin for this!" cried the iron hand of justice.

3

So Denny, once more in the street, leaned one hand against a dobe wall and tried to consider what he had seen and heard. It was all exceedingly odd; it was a little stranger than the episode of Joseph Simon and the imaginary portrait which was to be turned into real flesh and blood.

Was the Kid a nickname for an epidemic or a poison that everyone in this town dreaded and hated it so?

He went on down the street, wandering away from the hotel. A party of cowpunchers arriving in town with yells of jubilation, split through the gloom one by one on racing horses, waving their hats, screaming their shouts, and racing in a mad endeavor to reach the hotel first, and some forbidden prize which awaited them there.

But Si Denny did not see, and he heard only dull, dim sounds; so greatly was his mind employed upon the unraveling of his new mystery. Then a voice shrilled very close to him: "I'm the Kid!"

He whirled in amazement and joy, not unmixed with a little pang of awe. But there, in the middle of the street, stood a red-headed urchin surrounded by Mexican playmates and perhaps one or two sun-burned little Americans.

"I'm the Kid!" he shouted again. "You all try to catch me. I'm the Kid, till I'm caught!"

They started toward him with a joyous yell, rejoicing in their numbers, but the little redhead darted through them like a football star running through a broken field. He twisted and snaked here and there. Someone lunged straight at him— there was the crack of a hard little fist against flesh—a yell of pain—and the redhead was free and on the other side of the mob.

"I'm the Kid! You can't catch me! I'm the Kid!"

They raced at him with a shriek of fury and eagerness combined. He took to his heels. He doubled, he dodged through them. Crack—crack! His flying fists opened a gap, and he was through again, laughing until he reeled with the excess of his joy.

Then fate overtook him. The long arm of Denny shot out—the powerful hand of Denny fixed upon the nape of his neck. The redhead was lifted and tucked under Denny's arm. The rest of the little crowd rushed around Denny, whining with fury and clawing at the captive.

"Lemme go! Lemme go!" cried the redhead.

"What d'you want to do?"

"I want to beat in a few of their doggone faces."

"Keep away from him!" rumbled Si Denny.

The dread of his voice scattered the children. They fled and stood in frightened, inquisitive groups in the distance, kicking up dust with their bare toes, itching with hope that they might still be revenged upon their tormentor.

Upon the top of a crumbling dobe wall Si Denny deposited his captive.

"Well," he said, "you been raising the devil, ain't you?"

"Maybe so—maybe not," said the redhead.

"You know who I am?"

"Nope. I don't give a darn who you are."

"I'm the new deputy sheriff."

"That's a lie, and a loud one. Joe Belcher would never appoint a gent like you for such a job."

"Why not, you little snipe?"

"You got too much beef on you. You couldn't ride hosses through the mountains around here. You'd kill 'em off—doggone me if you wouldn't!"

Si Denny grinned, delighted by the shrewdness of this response.

"What's your name, kid?" he asked.

"First thing that comes handy."

"All right, boss. Who's this Kid that you been talking about to the rest of 'em?"

The little boy gaped at him. "Don't you know?"

"I'm asking you, son. Never mind what I know."

"Well," said the youngster, "doggone me if I ain't plumb tired of talkin', tonight. Particular about the Kid."

Si Denny took both the arms of the youngster. Redhead struggled fiercely, with an amazing, wiry strength. But the immense hands of Si were vises, and the arms of Red turned slowly back. His fists were tucked into the small of his back. Then they were pressed up higher and higher toward his shoulderblades.

"Will you talk now, you little pup?"

"No!" gasped out Red through set teeth.

"Now?"

"No, darn you! Darn you!"

Si Denny released the pressure suddenly. "You're a game kid," he announced without admiration, but as a fact worth stating.

He could feel the body of the child trembling with passion. Truly, in years to come, this would be a fighting cock of the walk! Then he drew out a pocketknife. It was a miracle of beauty. It had a pearl handle. It had five blades of the finest steel. He exposed it in his broad palm under the eyes of the child, and suddenly Red ceased trembling and wriggling and sighed.

"Jiminy!" said he.

"Look here," said Si Denny. He opened the main blade. It

was three and a half inches long. He picked up a piece of wood and slashed it through.

"My golly!" exclaimed Red.

"That's not all. Look here!"

There was a small blade—there was a nail file—there was a tiny corkscrew—there was even a little scissors.

"Take hold of it."

Red held forth two trembling hands. "Thanks," said he. "I won't drop it!"

He still held it in both hands. He dared not stir for fear the lovely vision should vanish.

"There ain't a knife in town like that!" he whispered.

"There ain't hardly one in the world like it," said Si Denny. "But look here, Red, that knife belongs to you."

"What!"

"I said that knife belongs to you."

Red trembled. "All right," he said huskily. "It's a pretty good joke, I guess."

Si Denny took the knife, closed the blades, and dropped it into the boy's pocket. Then he lifted him again by the nape of the neck and deposited him on the street.

"You're free, kid. That's your knife. Run away with it if you want to."

Red literally vanished into the night. But Si Denny knew men and women in this world; he even knew children! For he waited calmly at that place, and presently out of the darkness appeared the glowing head of Red.

He drifted about Si Denny in a circle, at a safe distance.

"How'd you know I'd come back?"

"I can tell a square shooter when I see one."

"That was a dirty trick—twisting my arms like that."

"That's why I gave you the knife."

Suddenly Red came up to him.

"Well," he said, "I don't owe you nothin'?"

"Not a thing."

"I keep the knife?"

"Sure."

There was a pause. He could feel, rather than see, how the eyes of Red increased in size.

"Well," said Red at length, "you want to know about the Kid, I guess?"

"That's it."

"I'm mighty sorry. I never seen him. Nobody else, hardly, ever seen him—I mean in this town."

"Except the sheriff?"

The boy chuckled. "Yep, the sheriff seen him. I guess the sheriff won't forget the day that he met up with the Kid. Jeff Hitchins seen him, too."

"Is Hitchins a big gent with a red face?"

"That's him. Always looks mad; nearly always *is* mad, too."

"Well, what do you know about the Kid? Where does he hang out? Near this town?"

"Jiminy, no! He hangs out everywhere!"

"No home?"

"Sure, his hoss is his home."

"I see," murmured Si. "He's an outlaw, eh?"

"You don't see right. He ain't no outlaw."

"Why don't he stay in one place, then?"

"No one place is good enough for the Kid, I guess."

Si Denny pondered. At the very moment when he came on the trail of his man, so it seemed, he found that the latter had turned into a will-o'-the-wisp. He might as well strive to come close to a thing made of thinnest air. In his bewilderment, he remembered that what the brain of a man cannot compass, the brain of a child can often achieve—through simplicity! He ceased his catechizing. He began to ask advice.

"Do me a favor, son," he said.

"Sure. Anything you say!" Red dropped a hand importantly upon his hip and waited for the query.

"I want to see the Kid."

"Well," said Red, "invite him into town."

"Who'll take the invitation to him?"

"I dunno. He'll hear about it. That's the way the Kid has. He hears things. Maybe he'll find out everything we said tonight. You can't tell about him. He's everywhere and nowhere at the same time!" He sighed in admiration.

"What'll make him want to come to town?"

"That's hard to say. You can't *make* him do nothin'."

"What does he want most in the world?"

"A fight," said Red instantly.

"He's a fighter, eh? Revolver?"

"Revolver, rifle, knife—there ain't nothin' that the Kid can't do! He'll run faster'n a sprinter and farther'n an Indian; he'll ride anything that walks on four feet; and he'll fight you with his bare fists or with a club—anything you want!"

"He's a killer, then?"

"Nope. he just fights to lay folks out when they think that they're as good as he is!"

"I understand. Then how'm I to get him to this town?"

The boy pondered. "You don't mind taking chances?" he said.

"I've taken chances before," said Si Denny, smiling faintly.

"Then you let folks know that you're here in town waiting for the Kid, and that if he's half a man, he'll come in to call on you, and when he comes in, you're going to fill him full of lead. You just tell somebody that."

"I'll tell you, Red. Will that do?"

"Sure it will! I'll fix it!"

"We'll let it go at that, then."

"So long, partner, and good luck! You sure got your nerve with you."

Red disappeared again, in that sudden way of which he was the complete and perfect master. The big man sauntered off down the street to turn again in his mind the strange events of the past few minutes. He strolled here and there and finally wandered back toward the hotel.

The first person he met in the lobby of the hotel was the big, red-faced cowpuncher, Hitchins, but Hitchins made no hostile movement toward him. Instead, the big fellow gaped at him with new eyes of amazement. Then he turned and whispered to his neighbor. The latter stared also toward Denny, and in a trice, every man in the room was watching and wondering.

There was no doubt that little Red had already done his work. He had transformed Si Denny into a hero with his report. Or, to look at it in another way, it was only necessary for the men of the town to know that he was challenging the Kid in order to make him a reputation as one in a thousand.

He had not been in his room for ten minutes when there was a tap on the doorm He opened it with caution, half expecting to find that volatile creature, the Kid, waiting outside. But it was the sheriff. He came in still panting with his haste.

"Didn't have no idea what you was driving at," he said eagerly to Si Denny. "Of course if I'd knowed that you was asking for that! While I'm not supposed to know that you're waiting to break the peace here by fighting with the Kid, I can't help telling you that I admire your nerve, and also that I got the price of your funeral if you don't have luck!"

This singular speech was listened to by Si Denny with no great reassurance.

"Look here," he asked sharply. "Why does everybody hate the Kid?"

"Why are *you* after him?" asked the sheriff.

"That's different. But most of you don't even know the Kid, or how he looks."

"That's just it. Take 'em by and large, folks hate things that they can't understand."

"I suppose so. How old do you make out the Kid to be?"

"I dunno. Maybe twenty. Maybe twenty-five."

It was just the age which Joseph Simon had demanded, and the heart of Si Denny grew warm. He was baiting this hook with his life, but he felt sure that if he could take the prize, it would be accepted by Simon. When he went to bed that night, it was to dream of fierce battles, of guns leveled in his face, and of the jar of challenging voices.

He wakened at the scratching of a match. He sat up in bed as the chimney was slipped down over his lamp and as its circular flame spread a glow through the room. Then he caught up his revolver from the chair where he had laid it in easy reaching distance before he closed his eyes. It was light, strangely light, and as he gripped it, the man of the painting stepped out before him from behind the lamp—the very same man had issued from the canvas, so it seemed, and stood before him.

The thin, handsome face, the bold eyes, and that narrow, fighting jaw were the same. There was only one difference, but this was something which could not have been hoped for—a small patch, as of a mole or a birthmark, which appeared high on the cheekbone, under the right eye of the man of the portrait.

"That gun is empty," said the Kid, and pointed to the floor.

The lightness of the weapon was explained to Si Denny, for he saw six long cartridges scattered there.

"I thought that we'd better talk a bit first," said the Kid.

"I didn't know," said Denny, "that you felt that way about such things."

"You've been misinformed," said the Kid without emotion. "I always like to know what a man is before I kill him."

"You aim to kill me, my friend?"

"Before morning—most certainly! But there is no hurry."

"I thought that you planned to drop a man and get him ready for a hospital instead of a grave."

"Of course," said the Kid, "killings are serious business. I can't afford it, usually. If you kill a man in a fair fight with a gun, his ghost is too apt to come back and use the hands of the law to kill you with a rope. I've always kept that in mind."

He spoke with a half sneer, slowly, and all the time measuring Si Denny with his eyes in a peculiar, inhuman fashion which made the flesh of the latter creep.

"But it's safe with you," continued the Kid.

"That makes me feel pretty comfortable," said Si Denny. "How do you figure that I'm any different from the rest?"

"That's easy," said the other, and he smiled with a gruesome glitter of eyes and teeth. "You come down here and tell people that you're gunning for me. That's enough all by itself. Then, you're a crook. When they look you up after you're bumped off, they'll be glad to know that you're on the minus side of the column."

'You know me, then?"

'I've heard about you."

"Tell me one thing, since I'm not to live to speak to any

other human being: Who brought the news to you about me?"

"Nobody. I saw you with Red, and I heard every word you said to him."

"How could you do that, man!"

"I was on the other side of the wall!"

It made Si Denny draw in his breath. He did not believe a word of this explanation, but it was so uncannily pat that it staggered him. After all, he had not thought to explore on the farther side of the fence while he was talking to Red. In his heart of hearts he wished that Joseph Simon and the matter of the portrait were at the bottom of the seven seas, but he called his best courage to his support.

"Tell me one thing more, my friend. Do you speak Spanish?"

That pleasant tongue came fluently from the lips of the Kid.

"I suppose I may say that I have the speech feeling for that language," he said modestly and in the most perfect Castilian.

"Then," said Si Denny, "I think that I can use you."

"You are quite wrong, sir. You cannot use me. I have no intention of accompanying you on the trip which you are about to make."

"I tell you, I haven't come here to fight."

"I am very sorry," said the Kid, and again that smile of infinite cruelty touched his lips.

A great fear rushed over Denny. He had no fear that he could handle men with persuasion, but this youngster was not human. He fell into a category of his own. But though the perspiration rushed out on the brow of Denny, he said quietly: "You are wrong, as I shall show you."

The Kid settled himself in a chair and rocked back in it.

"Good," he said with enjoyment. "You are about to bribe me. I shall listen to your offers."

"More money," said Si Denny, "than you ever before saw in all your life."

"Money? I have enough for my present uses. Money will not do it. You must bid higher than that for your life, Mr. Denny."

"I can do it. A strange adventure, I tell you, lies in wait for you if you will come with me."

The Kid hesitated an instant and then shook his head. "I have adventure enough," he said. "I enjoy myself very well, sir."

A sick sensation came over the heart of Si Denny, but still he persisted. He tried a last and desperate cast of the dice of this long chance.

"I will offer you," said he, "more danger than any one man ever before faced. That is my real bribe!"

The Kid paused again, shrugged his shoulders, and then a dreamy look came into his eyes. He sighed and looked yet again and with a new and gentler interest at Si Denny.

"Tell me about it," he said softly.

4

El Paso would by no means suit Joseph Simon as the place of rendezvous. He answered the long and cautiously worded wire of Si Denny with a telegram instructing the latter to meet him at an obscure shack among the foothills of the Diablo range. There, at the appointed hour, repaired the discoverer. He found that Halsey and Marmont were waiting for him at the spot, a disgruntled pair who favored him with sardonic smiles, however, when they saw him swing out of the saddle and enter the old shack unaccompanied.

"Where is Monsieur le Diable?" asked Marmont. "I had a wire from Simon to come back just when I was about to put my hands on a man who would have looked the part of the picture so well that the painter would have thought him his own idea turned into flesh and blood."

"I was even nearer," said Halsey with a sigh. "I had

bought two railroad tickets instead of one. Then came Simon's wire and found me as I was about to start for the train!''

To these assertions Denny returned an ironical smile and complimented them upon their good fortune.

"But where," asked Marmont again, "is the man you promised to bring?"

"On the way, I hope," said Denny.

"You left *that* to chance?" they asked him, amazed, and he could only shrug his shoulders.

"Who is the man?" queried Halsey.

"Marmont named him," replied Si Denny. "He is the devil. He told me he would come; I couldn't press the point. One doesn't strike close bargains or get signed contracts from the devil!"

That was all the satisfaction which he would give them.

In the meantime, Joseph Simon was hurrying toward the place of the appointed rendezvous as fast as he could, though this was at no round pace, for he was no expert horseman, and he was already so racked by the long journey that every joint of his meager frame cried out against speed. He gritted his teeth, however, and made on at a steady jog trot, keeping his eyes fastened far ahead of him with a look of unutterable expectation and anxiety, as though he would draw the blue Diablo range closer to him.

It rolled near, at last, but still there were some weary miles before him. He had dipped out of a hollow and mounted to the low rim on the farther side when there was a sound of scattering gravel beneath the hoofs of a horse behind him. He glanced back in alarm, and there he saw a youth of between twenty and twenty-five years, finely mounted on a black horse—a youth beneath whose wide-brimmed sombrero he saw the very face of his portrait looking forth at him. Joseph Simon, uttering a shrill cry, threw up his hands with a gesture of wonder and delight and almost of fear, as though he felt that there might be something unearthly in this incarnation of an idea.

"The kind God," cried Simon, striking his hands together now, "the kind God has brought you to me. I give Him thanks!"

"Thank Denny," said the Kid, drawing rein when his big black horse was very near. Then he sat in his saddle and eyed Simon up and down in that incredibly insolent and self-assured manner of his.

That very manner, however, seemed to add to the delight of Simon, who nodded his joy, and when he was able to speak again exclaimed: "Señor Vereal, it is fate, not any man, which accomplishes such meetings!"

"My name," said the Kid coldly as ever, "is not Vereal."

"Ah?" said Simon, somewhat taken aback. "It is not? But perhaps not," he added, with a little, regretful sigh, peering more closely under the shadow of the other's hat. "Perhaps you do not wear that name. My own is Joseph Simon; may I ask for yours, sir?"

He had spoken all of this in Spanish, and in the same tongue the Kid answered: "Some call me the Kid. That will do very well. Now, Mr. Simon, what will you have of me?"

Caution, however, had taken the place of the first delight of Joseph Simon. He continued to smile, but with a greater reserve.

"What should I have to do with you, sir, except to bid you good day? I mistook you for another man—a Vereal, in fact."

The Kid smiled and shrugged his shoulders. "However," he remarked, "I think that Denny didn't lie to me."

"Did a Mr. Denny tell you that I wished to see you?" asked Simon, frowning.

"He did not."

"I do not understand then, why—"

"I saw the other three go for the shack. I've been waiting here since morning to see them go by. None of them would do. I knew that there was some one still behind the deal. But when I saw you, I knew that it was time to talk. So here we are!"

"What three?" asked Joseph Simon, with perfect blankness.

"That is a question," said the Kid. "Also, what have you in the saddlebag? That is another question."

Joseph Simon grew pale and clutched instantly at the little flat leather pouch which he had been endeavoring to conceal by pressing his knee over it.

"It is nothing," he said with violence.

The smile of the Kid was almost a grin. "Now, Mr. Simon," he said, "what do you want with me?"

"We will talk in the house," urged Simon.

"Where you have three men and three guns waiting. No, this will do me for a room, and a saddle is good enough for a chair."

Simon shifted himself in the leather with a groan, as though he were far from agreeing with his companion. Then he looked about him to the far-off pale circle of the horizon, and there was nothing in between to fill his eyes except the heat waves shimmering and dancing over the surface of the desert and the stiff-standing Spanish daggers everywhere.

"Tell me first," said Simon, "why you thought that none of the three would do. Tell me that, young man?"

"I have no money," said the Kid readily. "Why should they want me?"

The simplicity with which he answered made Joseph Simon smile, but a moment later he sighed.

"We are in the hands of God," he said, "to do with as He will. Come, then! Since there is no better way, we shall talk here, although this hideous sun burns all thought out of my brain. I had hoped that I might come to know you better before I confided in you, but since I cannot do that, I shall tell you everything at once.

"First, then, there is in old Mexico, within sixty miles of the border, something of great value which belongs to me and which I wish to take out."

"Then why not go to get it?"

"Because if I went in person, a thousand men would join the hunt to find me. I could not live for a day below the Rio Grande."

"You want me to do that work, then?"

"Exactly."

"I am no sneak thief, Mr. Simon."

"This thing which I speak of could only be carried by a hundred mules."

At this, the Kid sat up in his saddle. He swung a leg over

the horn of his saddle, rolled a cigarette, and sat sidewise, listening with a devout interest to this startling statement.

"A hundred mules, then," said he, "are to be brought with heavy loads, from some place sixty miles south of the border. Is that it?"

"It is."

"You need an army, not one man."

"You are wrong. An army could do nothing. There is only one man in the world who could help me. You are that man, my friend!"

"Maybe," said the Kid nonchalantly. "How am I to do it?"

"First," said Simon, "I must know that you will try the thing before I go deeper."

"What will make me want to?"

"For you, fifty thousand dollars in cash the moment the thing which is mine is brought to me."

"Fifty thousand for me—a million for you, eh?"

"Of course," said Simon with astonishing frankness. "Much more than a million, too. Could I afford, otherwise, to hire four men for this work? First of all, I must pay you enough to make you wish to be honest with me. Even granting that you are devoted heartily to my service, my young friend, the odds are still only one in ten that I shall win. In the meantime, I pay you all of your expenses, and—what will you have by the week or the month?"

"Nothing."

"What do you say?"

"I work for fifty thousand—not by the day. Now the game?"

"That is a story. But I have your word, then, señor? You are my man, to try this thing after you have heard the story—or if when you have heard it you decide to refuse, you swear to me that the story I am to tell you will never be repeated?"

For response, the Kid thought for a moment, and then proffered his hand. It was shaken with a sort of grave delight by the other man who then mopped his forehead and drew a great breath.

''The first step is the greater half of the journey,'' he said as much to himself as to his friend.

While they talked, their horses had been walking slowly on, and now they came to a great outcropping of rocks on a hilltop and Simon suggested that they sit here in the shade while the rest of the plan was unraveled.

''For when a horse is beneath one,'' he said, ''how can one think?''

At this, the Kid chuckled, and, dismounting from their saddles, they sat down in the black shade and took off their hats to the coolness of the wind across the desert. The Kid rolled another cigarette; Simon took from a long golden case a thin, black cigar.

As he slowly puffed, he half closed his eyes with the enjoyment of that delicious Havana. Not even the strangeness of the story which he told could divert him from that full epicurean satisfaction. The Kid lolled upon one elbow, stretched at full length and seemingly watching the desert with a greater interest than the face of the narrator.

At times, indeed, he even looked quite away, and, raising his head, would stare into the pale blue sky where a buzzard traced wide circles upon tireless wings.

5

''Do you know Mexico?'' asked Joseph Simon.

''I've known Mexicans,'' answered the Kid.

''In the States?''

''Yes.''

''Then you don't know them at all. If you put a wolf in a cage or a bear in a park behind bars, you have no idea of what they are. People in strange countries are like fish out of water. The Mexicans are more so than others.

"They need a language which will flow like water. They must be among people who do not laugh at gestures. Besides, most of the Mexicans in the States are of the peon class. They represent Mexico no more than Norman peasants illustrate the refinements of the Parisian French. But you must know that though the Rio Grande is a muddy little stream, yet it is one of the greatest boundaries in the world.

"North of it El Paso is as modern as any American city; on the other side of the water, Juarez is still half asleep in the middle ages. A poor century for sleep, you may say, but Mexico has her charms. Some people never learn them. But you will, my young friend. You have enough brains to understand what the fools cannot see. Very well, I am not giving you a lecture on geography and Mexican manners, but this leads up to another matter.

"You have read a little history, I presume?" He cocked his head upon one side and snapped out the words at the Kid.

"I've read a little," admitted the latter.

"What is your picture of a medieval town?"

"A castle on a cliff, I suppose, and a village gathered around its feet. Is that what you mean?"

"Just so! Just so! By the way, by what name am I to know you?"

At this, the Kid paused for a moment, as though this simple question were a weighty matter. At length he said: "You may call me John Jones, if you wish."

"You belong, I see, to a large and often distinguished family, Mr. Jones," said Simon with twinkling eyes.

The Kid, or rather, John Jones, shrugged his shoulders and disdained even a glance at the face of his companion.

"To come back to the story, Mr. Jones," said the other, "your picture of the town of the middle ages is just what I had in mind. Now I ask you to conceive the Mexican town of San Triste. Its population is of some ten or twelve thousand. It is situated in a rich district. Even its poor are not really poor, compared with those of some Mexican towns. There are many old families, rich in Spanish blood, but, rich and poor and middle classes, the town of San Triste, in the old days—say a dozen years ago—was gathered at the feet of one name, and that name was Vereal.''

At this, John Jones cast a sharp glance at his companion. He encountered an equally sharp scrutiny on the part of the other.

''That's an odd name,'' murmured John Jones.

''Very odd, as you say,'' said Simon. ''The family was an extremely ancient one. How far it may be traced back in Spain, I cannot tell, but at least it was of importance there before the discovery of America. Vereal came out with Cortez. He became distinguished for his services, particularly in the fighting about the City of Mexico, and in the last long siege where they won the city street by street and island by island, no one's sword ran red more often than did that of this Vereal.

''Of course he was rewarded like the rest of the conquistadores. But he differed from them in this—that while they spent as freely as they earned, most of them, Vereal knew how to improve what was given him. He created a great estate. Finally, when all of Mexico was subdued, he transferred his holdings to the district of San Triste.

''The Vereals remained there from that date. For more than three and a half centuries they were princes in that land. They built churches, saved the hungry in times of famine by their largess out of their big granaries, covered the hills with their flocks and herds, built and owned whole villages, and were, in short, like barons of those old Dark Ages.''

He made a pause in order to puff carefully at his cigar, which had almost gone out. After that, he began again, and continued the narrative.

''Who can continue in prosperity through thirty-five or forty decades? Not even the Vereals could do so. If there were ever a revolution, they stood for the old order. They fought for Spain when Mexico was about to become free, and of course they lost a great deal in that way. So it was, always. The men of the Vereal name were always very gallant and very true, but they were always very foolish. Their great estate was whittled away and whittled away!''

He sighed in the greatest sadness.

"What one good businessman could have done, even if there had been only one in every other generation, who can say? But in nearly four hundred years they did nothing to build up what they had received from their first ancestor. They still were spending. Perhaps you will even wonder that there was anything left? But there was much left—very much indeed!

"There were still mines in the mountains. There were still plantations by the river. There were still ranches in the hills. Since some things can never be destroyed, for there is always a return, all the millions which the Vereals had so carelessly and so recklessly and so generously wasted came back in this: They had a new empire in the hearts of the people of San Triste.

"If a fire gutted a poor man's house, his starving family was brought into a new house and fed and clothed by the Vereals. The father was equipped to begin again where he left off. Sometimes a rich man failed in his business. Perhaps he was new in San Triste. But if he were an honest man and a good man, it did not matter how many sins of business folly he had heaped upon his head. The Vereal money chests were open to his hungry hands. He did not need to leave San Triste.

"You will begin to wonder that for four hundred years one family could still produce men so good and so generous as these men of the house of Vereal. But I do not mean that they were all good and that they were all generous. You must simply consider that in the family of Vereal, San Triste was a religion. The streets on which they walked have been paved by one ancestor. The church in which they prayed had been built by another.

"Do you comprehend? You might say that in serving the people of that place they were serving themselves. Besides, for hundreds of years they had been taught to regard money as dirt. The current coin which was passed from hand to hand, by them, was the worship, the love, the fear of the people.

"In how many ways they possessed that town, I cannot tell

you. But I know that when a child was born to the name of Vereal, the whole city came to sing and dance and make a carnival. They walked all the way from the heart of the town and up the hill and into the great patio of the Vereal house. There wine and beer were served to them freely. For twenty-four hours they thought of nothing but play.

"But if a Vereal died, the whole town was instantly in mourning. When the funeral procession began, the men of San Triste walked behind the body, and the women and children kneeled by the side of the road while the chief officials of the city carried the bier.

"You see why I say, then, that a Vereal who spent money on this place spent money on himself. It was true that they remained public benefactors, but then they received more than real homage from the citizens. They had power—great power!

"Once a rebellion started in the province. A detachment was thrown out toward San Triste. A thousand soldiers gathered in the Plaza Municipal, and their leaders made speeches to the people and told them to come into the ranks and join the new order which was sure to prevail.

"Word of this came to Señor Vereal—Diego Vereal, that was. He took his cane, for he was a very old man. He hobbled into the Plaza Municipal. He raised his cane. People turned to him. Those near him fell on their knees so that those farther away could hear him and see him.

"He only said: 'These men are foolish. Do not listen to them.'

"Then he went home, and in five minutes the soldiers found their guns torn out of their hands, their uniforms in rags, their captains in jail, and they themselves hustled into the country."

"Well," said John Jones, "that was as good as having an army of his own, eh?"

"By all means. Better, because it was really cheaper in the long run. I could tell you much more. A bandit once kidnaped the son of a rich man in San Triste. The rich man went to Vereal and begged for his help. Vereal stood up in church the next Sunday and said to the people: 'There are among you

some who know the man Grenacho. He has taken away the
son of a man in San Triste. Let word be taken to Grenacho
that this man is my friend and that his son is as dear to me as
my own son.'

"After that he sat down and said no more. You will
understand, my friend, that Grenacho was a terrible man. He
was a lion. Aye, for that matter, he still is one. He has shed
blood as one pours out pulque which is old and spoiled. He
has murdered men for the sake of a copper coin. He has
murdered them for diversion, when he was weary of the day.
Such a man was this Grenacho. He had about him a strong
band of ruffians who would fight to the death at his bidding.

"What hold, will you say, did Vereal have on such a man?
Only this—Grenacho was born in San Triste and therefore he
belonged to Vereal. A week later, the young man was
returned to San Triste. His name was Francisco Cabrero. I
well remember the day he appeared in the town, pale and
thin. He went to the house of Vereal and dropped on his
knees and tried to kiss the hands of old Don Diego.

" 'Hush, child,' said the old man, 'Thank me no more than
you would thank your father.'

"Nevertheless, it was a lucky day for Grenacho when he
returned Don Francisco safe and sound. For he himself, the
very next year, was taken and brought to San Triste and tried
for his life and, of course, judged to death.

"On the day when his sentence was to be pronounced, he
was advised to remind the Vereal that he had once served his
family and done their bidding. He sent that message. Old
Don Diego was dead, but his young son, Pedro, was there.
He was newly back from Paris to take his place as the head of
the family, and I very well can remember how the messenger
was brought in to him.

"The poor fellow had been bribed to carry the word. He
stood with his hat in his hand at the farther end of the room
and dared not lift his head. He murmured his words. A mozo
had to repeat them. When Don Pedro heard, he said: 'Is this
true? Has Grenacho served me?'

" 'Yes,' said the mozo. 'Last year he did the bidding of
your father in a small matter.'

" 'It is enough,' said Don Pedro.

"He ordered his carriage and was driven to the place where the judgment was about to be rendered. He came only to the door of the great room and said no more than this: 'I desire that this man, Grenacho, shall go free.'

"You will think that this was a great deal to do, even for a Vereal. Believe me, Mr. John Jones, within five minutes Grenacho was at liberty. He was given a horse and decent clothes. He went to the house of Vereal and stood before young Don Pedro. I was at that time present, and I shall never forget.

"This Grenacho, you will understand, is a huge man with a long, thin mustache. He looks as terrible and as strong and as swift as a great cat. He was very proud, also. He stood with his arms folded across his breast and started to thank Don Pedro for his life. But Don Pedro would not listen.

"He raised a hand, and having stopped the other, he spoke as follows: 'I am told that you are a great rascal, Grenacho. I hear that you have done many things, and that among others, you have taken the lives of men of San Triste. Do not answer. Do not speak a syllable! You are living, and let that be enough, but now go and never again while there is life in you, set foot in the district of San Triste. Begone!'

"For my part, I looked to see Grenacho draw a gun and murder Don Pedro, but instead, he bowed almost to the floor and backed away through the door. From that day to this, he has never dared to come within twenty miles of the town."

6

Here Simon made a pause in his recital, nodding quietly to himself and smiling with reminiscent eyes as he recalled the picture which that scene had made. If he waited for John Jones to make a comment upon this strange story, however, he waited in vain, for that young worthy was at the moment contemplating the matchless ease of the flight of the carrion bird far above his head.

"Perhaps," continued Joseph Simon, at last, "you will be wondering what was my place in the house of Vereal, that I should have seen so much of the life of the family. I shall tell you freely.

"I have already said that the extravagance of the family was like the extravagance of a line of kings. With such habits, there was a need for a great deal of ready cash.

"There were not only the charities in San Triste to deal out, but there were also other great expenses. Every son of the family, you must know, would have his education completed in a great university in a foreign land. Everyone must have his excursions abroad, and wherever they moved, they must have a valet, a secretary or two, a business representative, a majordomo of the household, a special chef, and others—together with servants of the servants.

"Whenever a Vereal bought a racehorse or a yacht or a house in Madrid or in Florence, every person in San Triste rubbed his hands and read about the details of the new purchase, and enjoyed it all just as much as though he were at that instant lounging in the pleasure gardens or sitting on the deck of the yacht.

"Such habits even a millionaire could not endure. The Vereals fell into debt. They fell deeper and deeper into debt. At length, their creditors became pressing for quick payment, for there were so many of them and each had claims so large and often so ill-defined that it was thought perhaps the debts might be greater than the property.

"Vereal—this was old Don Diego—could not tell what to do. Then one of his creditors came to him and said as follows: 'Let me pay all of the other debts which now trouble you. You will then owe money to one person only—which will be myself. When that state is arrived at, you need concern yourself only with paying the interest on those debts for some years until you are able to begin paying off the capital.'

"This was generous talk, you will say. But then, it was talk from the lips of a generous man—and that was my father, Jacob Simon. The Vereal could not help but listen. He agreed, and my father began to pay the debts and take the notes of the Mexican. The debts were very large. They were so great, indeed, that in the end my father had to sell many great properties in order to pay them; he had to strip himself of all of his other interests, and in the end he found that he possessed nothing in the world of true value except the notes of the Vereal, and those notes were for no less than two millions and six hundred thousands of dollars."

He finished the naming of this huge sum with a voice which rang with an earnest excitement, but still John Jones made no answer, nor so much as turned to look into the face of the narrator.

"Of course something had to be done at once. The Vereal heard the full amount of the debts named off to him in a lump sum without the slightest emotion. He called for his head secretary into whose hands the majority of the business affairs of the family were placed.

" 'I owe a debt of about three million—a little more or a little less,' said he. 'I wish to pay it at once. Let something be sold.'

"The secretary did not dare to tell him that if he tried to realize three million dollars with a quick sale, he perhaps would become bankrupt. Afterward he came to my father and asked him for aid. My father already knew all the facts. Of course you may be sure that he had gone over every inch of the property before he began to accept the debts against it.

"It had a value, including all the mining claims, the cattle ranches, the flocks of sheep, the buildings in San Triste, and the rich farms in the river bottoms, of about five million and a half. But a quick sale would not bring in half of the true value. The mines, for instance, would have to be disposed of for next to nothing.

"When the secretary ran over these facts, he said it was what he expected. He dared not face the Vereal with such news. So my father took that duty on his shoulders. He went to the Vereal and said to him: 'Señor Vereal, we have looked over the resources of the estate and we find that a quick sale of all of the Vereal properties would indeed pay your debts but would leave you, also, no better than a ruined man.'

"The Vereal answered without the slightest hesitation: 'Let everything be sold, then, and the proceeds placed in your hands. If there is enough to pay you, I am satisfied. If there is more, I shall be happy to have it. If there is less than enough, I shall go to work with my own hands to make the money to pay you.'

"This was the fashion in which a Vereal spoke. My father felt as though he had degraded a king by even listening to such words. He went back to his house, very worried. He was troubled at the thought that so old and great an estate— this strange little kingdom of the Vereal—was about to be dissolved, and indirectly through the agency of debts due to him.

"I will tell you truly that he loved the Vereal and their history. He worked day and night, trying to see a way out of this matter, but he could find none. He grew more and more nervous as the time went on, and finally he fell into a quick fever. It was his brain, do you see? He died in two days, and left me to take his place at that very critical time.

"Luckily, I knew everything. Besides, I had not come to be so much afraid of the Vereal as other people were. I am, in fact afraid of nothing,'' said Joseph Simon. ''People cannot overawe me!''

John Jones, perhaps, recalled the first moments of his meeting with Simon, but he did not smile.

"At least," said Simon, "I was able to go straight to the Vereal and sit down with him. I said to him: 'You feel that you are doing a very fine thing in selling your property to pay your debts to me. As a matter of fact, you are doing an injury to me. I do not think that you will be able to sell your property for more than five-sixths of what you owe to me.'

" 'Is not that enough?' said the Vereal to me.

" 'Every dollar that I have loaned to you, returned with the proper interest—that alone is enough for me!' said I.

"He sat up in his chair and stared at me as though I were a plague turned into the form of a man. However, I did not mind his contempt. I was working for his own good far more than for mine.

" 'Besides,' said I, 'though it may please you to be done with this whole money tangle, you are not fair to your children. What will they think of you when they find that you shuffled away a burden from your shoulders and so left them penniless?'

" 'You will pass to another subject,' said the Vereal. 'In the Vereal family the honor of a father is the honor of a son. Have no care for the desires of my boy. He shall see nothing except as I see it.'

" 'But,' said I, 'there is a solution for the whole problem.'

" 'I am listening,' said he, still sneering.

" 'Take a ship and go to Europe,' said I. 'Take a two-year or a three-year jaunt abroad.'

" 'I would to heaven that I could,' said Don Pedro.

" 'It can be done,' said I.

" 'By a bankrupt man? I shall not cheat my creditors,' said he.

" 'I shall myself be able to furnish the money and you will be able yourself to pay me all the interest that I require.'

"He shook his head, at that, to indicate that the matter was too strange for him to understand.

" 'You must simply give up the old life for a few years,'

said I. 'And after you have done that, you may return to it as soon as you will please to do so. For a few years spend like a man who is only rich—not like a king. After that, I guarantee that you may be the king again.'

"He asked me how that could be, and I told him that instead of taking a dozen attendants for himself and another half dozen for his son when they went abroad, they must go with only two—a valet for himself and a tutor for his son. They must take care of themselves as well as they could, but they must guarantee that they would give no money away. I made no other limitations.

"The Vereal listened to me, and he made a wry face, but he nodded. 'Something is better than nothing,' said he.

"Then I went on to detail the rest of the plan. It was not a very new or a brilliant one. It was simply that it had not occurred to my father, for otherwise he should have been able to carry it through. I proposed that the entire management of the estate be turned over into my hands with authority to buy and sell, hire and discharge, make contracts or purchase anything in the name of Vereal from a gold mine to a set of mule harness.

"I proposed, in a word, that the Vereal should have one or two hired men in whom he could trust and who would keep in touch with every move I made concerning the management of the property. After that arrangement had been made, I could take complete charge of the establishment—the ranches, the mines, the farms—and all the other items in that estate. I would endeavor to show him what good management could accomplish within a few years.

"The Vereal listened to this proposal with great interest. He told me to draw up a power of attorney as complete and as sweeping as I chose to make it. I did so, and made out a document by which I could, if I wished, transfer his whole estate to my pocket and walked away with it while he was abroad. He gave it to his lawyer to read when I brought it the next day. The lawyer turned white when he passed his eye through the items. 'If you sign this,' he said to the Vereal, 'you have given away your birthright!'

" 'Good,' said the Vereal, and he instantly caught up the

paper and scratched his name at the bottom of the last page. He gave it to me. 'There will be no spies of mine to overlook your work,' he said. 'I shall trust you with everything. You are the master, my friend Simon!' said he.

"A day later, he had sailed for Europe and left all of his little kingdom in my hands!"

7

At this point John Jones, as he chose to call himself, interrupted for the first time.

"This is a fairy tale," he said.

"It is better," said Simon. "It is a fairy tale which is true. Consider, then, what would happen in a book of fiction if the poor, extravagant Spaniard entrusted all of his estate in the hands of the wicked, the grasping Simon!"

"It would never be believed," said John Jones without emotion.

"It would not," said Joseph Simon in a trembling voice. "But I shall tell you what Simon did!"

He had finished his first cigar, but as the relish of what he had accomplished in the old days came back upon his mind, he selected from the case a second cigar and lighted it with his usual care. When the fragrant blue-brown smoke was curling about his head, he continued his story.

"I had, of course, a list of all the holdings. I began at the top of the list and went through to the bottom. I started with the farms. I found at once that the farms were operated by old retainers of the family. In the entire list there was not one who really understood farming. There had been no rotation of crops, no care to secure modern machinery for cultivation. Vineyards ran wild; orange groves were half decayed.

"Of course I discharged all of these men from their places. I brought into the work experts who had been trained in agricultural colleges. There was an instant change. Land which had grown a scant three sacks to the acre the year before, produced in the next ten and twenty sacks.

"I tell you this simply as an example. I shut up the great house in San Triste. I discharged the host of parasites who clustered there. I used only three rooms—one was for the kitchen, one for my sleeping chamber, one for my dining and living room and office. A cook and a secretary were all I kept of all the list of useless people who had been there before.

"I went on from the management of the house and of the farm lands to other things. I looked into the cattle ranches. Just such people as had run the farms were now running the ranches. They were discharged, of course. Other men were substituted who understood the complicated problems of breeding and feeding. The first year the returns were slow, but in the second year they were a miracle!

"I went on to the mines, and there I found the worst conditions of all. Men went out to the mines knowing nothing of how they should be managed, and there was a general system of pillage. On one mine there was an actual loss for the working of it. I thought it must be closed down.

"But after I had put in a competent engineer, what result was there, do you think? I shall tell you! That mine was opened out, and new drifts were sunk into the mountainside. In a single short fortnight it began to pay, above all expenses, at the rate of twenty thousand dollars a month!

"But I could tell you all of today and all of tomorrow of the things which I accomplished. In short, within the first year, I discovered that the first valuation of the property, though based honestly enough on the actual income which the Vereal was deriving from it, was totally inadequate. Whereas it had been put down at five and a half millions as the actual worth of the total estate, within a single year I had raised the income to a million pesos and more. But that was not all. I discovered that I could still increase the income.

"Having taken in, as I say, a big million in profits in that first year, I dumped it back, every cent, into the operation. I retained not a cent of the interest upon my own two million and a half. Not even that was considered. For you must see, my friend, that I was determined to perform a miracle for the benefit of the Vereal.

"The first year was a great and a strange one, as I have said, but before it ended, I began to have much trouble. The people I had displaced nourished the fiercest hatred against me. Before three months elapsed, two bullets were fired at me, and a fanatic attempted to stab me while I was asleep. Such things were terrible to me. I am not a very brave man in the face of such dangers, señor.

"But I could not give up my great work. I hired a bodyguard of four courageous and gallant men. They gave me shelter. Two of them were constantly at my side while the other two slept. In this way, I was fairly safe, but still, I knew that a chance bullet might be the end of me at any time.

"Then came a stern letter from the Vereal saying that he had received many complaints and that everyone I had displaced must be reinstated. I answered him at once that he had given me full charge and that I intended to use it. But I saw that I must do something. My heart bled. Therefore I determined to grant a pension to each of those whom I had displaced. I made the pensions as low as I could, but each was enough for the wretches to live on, in addition to what other income they had from money pilfered while they were in the service of the Vereal.

"How much, do you think, was I compelled to disburse in this fashion during the second year of my stewardship? I tell you, John Jones, that my heart aches to think of it. No less than three hundred thousand dollars were spent in that fashion! A third of a million thrown away.

"You would think that the pensioners would be grateful for the money which they now received without even a pretense of work! No, no! No gratitude! Only hatred because they had been displaced. I could not show my face in the streets of San Triste, I was so raged at and cursed. For the sake of my life, I had to enter and leave the town in the dead of the night, by swift horses! But still I stuck at the post. They were bitter days and often at night I could not sleep for fear. But fear could not drive me away. I remained, and the miracle continued to be worked.

"I have said that at the end of the first year there was a million of profit. What think you of the second year? The reinvested million was returned, and another million was added to it!

"Then a childish, a foolish thought came to me. I swore to myself that when the Vereal returned to his home, I should be able to say to him: 'When you left San Triste, you owed more than you were worth at the moment. Now behold what a change!' As part of this scheme, I began to bring money shipments in hard cash to the old house in San Triste. Ah, now you raise your head, John Jones. It is true. This is the part of the tale which will most interest you. Mule loads of silver were brought. They were carted away again to be shipped; but not all was shipped.

"Out of every cargo brought in on mule back, guarded by the muleteers and our own hired soldiers, some heavy portions were conveyed by two old servants whom I had brought to the place, down into the deep interior of the house to a secret region which, so far as I knew, had been forgotten by all living men and which had been discovered by me only when I set about finding a place to secrete this treasure.

"In the meantime, my troubles gathered. Letters began to arrive from the Vereal. For the pensioners and the townsfolk of San Triste had finally formed a mission and sent three representatives to Switzerland, where the Vereal was living with his little son, his sole heir and the last of the race.

"Now Don Pedro commanded me to give over my new and foolish methods, to restore the old retainers to their former positions. I could only answer, as I saw my work tottering to a sudden fall, that he had given me authority for three years, and that the third year was hardly begun. I would hold fast to my authority to the very end.

"That was what I did, at great cost of danger, God knows, and in constant dread of every day. I increased my diligence. I prepared for the great accounting which I would make to Don Pedro. Let him rave and rage now if he chose. In the end, I could make all well. That I was confident of.

"I began to collect in that deep and secret subterranean chamber great deposits of treasure. Not suddenly, but every day of the year something was added. I reduced the bulk. I converted silver, in large part, into gold and into jewels, easily transportable. Things which the eye could grasp at a glance! So the year wore away, and at last the day of Don Pedro's return came.

"It was a great festival in San Triste, you may be sure. The people came to the house, the night before, and filled the patio, cursing me, and promising me that my time had come and that I should answer for the evil I had done. The evil I had done! Well, well, I sat in the house and smiled as I listened!

"The next day, Don Pedro came. I could follow his progress to the house by the shouts of the crowd. Through a window, I saw him come into the great patio, big as the court of a king's palace, surrounded by the people. They were weeping and singing and calling him father. They had taken his little son of ten years, young Don José, upon their shoulders.

"Then I went back to my room and waited. Finally Don Pedro came, alone. He greeted me with a black brow.

" 'You have done much harm to my children in San Triste,' he said. 'Now, Joseph Simon, we will make an end quickly. The estate will be sold within the month, and you shall be paid.'

"I bowed to him and said that I wished to make to him my accounting. I then laid before him sheets in which there were presented the lists of income under his old régime and then under mine. It was seen, then, that whereas four hundred thousand pesos was the greatest amount he had ever received in a single year from his property, under my stewardship the sum had been increased to—what will you say? No, my young friend, you will not believe me when I say it, but the truth was that in the third year, two million and a half, almost to a cent, had been brought in, and in the two years preceding another two million and a half had been brought into the coffers and had been expended again in improvements.

"I told him, and it was the truth, that he could go to his

mines and find them operating with the finest modern machinery—all paid for in full. That he could go to his cattle ranches and find them stocked with the best grades of cattle, and these twice as numerous as his old herds of skinny cows.

"I could tell him these wonderful truths and bid him go forth to look to make sure for himself. But when I had ended he only said: 'Listen to me, Joseph Simon! I had rather have all my farms swept with fire than that my wealth should have been made to grow by the misery of my children!'

"I was staggered and crushed. But still I had one recourse. I said: 'Come with me. You have still something to see with your own eyes!' "

8

"I led him down to the cellar of the house. I carried him down to a second level, far below the street, where the air was cold and the masonry was wet with the sweating. But still I brought him lower and so, at the last, down a flight of steps and winding into a deeper chamber beneath all the rest. How it ever came there, or how many more like it there may be mined into the rocks under the place where the Casa Vereal stands, I cannot guess.

"Perhaps in the old dark days of the conquistadores, they needed secret retreats where enemies could be carried for torture or for long confinement, or where they could retreat in time of need.

"At any rate, I brought him into a chamber of his own house of whose existence he himself had known nothing before. I showed him a number of stout chests standing there. The timber had been carried down by my two trusted servants, and they had built the chests, securing the boards with heavy screws, and binding the boxes with iron. I opened the chests one by one with my keys, and in every one there was a treasure. I let him look, I listened to his exclamations, and his wonder was a delight to me.

"Then I said: 'Señor, you see before you fifty mule loads of silver worth a quarter of a million in coined money. Yonder is gold which will load twenty mules, worth more than fifteen hundred thousand dollars. In this inner chest—look for yourself!'

"I opened it to him. The casket was filled to the brim with fine jewels, all of great price—pearls and rubies and green emeralds and diamonds of the finest water. I could say to him: 'I have showed you the account of my stewardship, señor. I have showed you that your income is now quintupled through my management.

"'Your lands are freed from debt, and in this chamber there is enough treasure to pay the old debts to the last dollar. I show you this not because I wish to take the money, but to let you know that if I am continued in this stewardship, all of this money will be assigned to you, and I shall take for my payment only a percentage interest in your estate and make only this term: That I be allowed to continue in full charge of all your properties.'

"He waited and said nothing. I went on: 'If San Triste cries out against me, why should that trouble the Vereal? He can return to Europe. I shall guarantee to him an income of two million every year. My own profit will be what I make above that sum!'

"It was a proud moment for me, to be able to justify myself in this fashion, but the Vereal only smiled. 'By your lights,' he said, 'you have acted well. I presume that I should even thank you for it. But for the money, Simon, has been wrung out from the sufferings of my children. It is hateful to me. All must be restored to the old order. If this money will repay you, take it all, and God be with you!'

"'In the name of heaven,' I said to him, 'will you restore everything to the old tenants? But they are ignorant! They do not know even the management of the machinery which I have installed in the mines and on the farms. All will be lost!'

"He only said: 'My mind is as fixed as a rock. Let no

more be said. I shall give you a few days to terminate your connection with my estate. Then you may take your treasure, here, and go. You have worked hard and honestly, I have no doubt. But you have taken money, which is dirt, in exchange for the tears of my people, which are more precious than jewels to me.'

"What could I say to such a madman? I went to my room in despair and threw myself upon a couch and wept like a child. But there was no changing his mind. He would not even talk again of the thing, and I determined to do as he bade me do. I finished my accounts. I added the last sum. I left my stewardship accounted for to the final penny; I struck the last balance, and then I prepared to remove the money which belonged to me.

"Then came the catastrophe. I have told you that, in the days of old Don Diego, he had quelled an uprising by his mere presence in the town. But there were still the seeds of a revolution germinating in the mountains and in other districts where the name of Vereal was hardly known. Now they had heard of the absence of the Vereal, of the hatred of the people for the steward he had left behind him when he went away.

"At the same time, a new revolution having been planned—you yourself are old enough to remember it—a force of the men who wished to fight for a new order, swept suddenly down from the mountains and came upon San Triste. They learned, when they came, that the Vereal had returned, but that could not stop them. They went on. The Vereal, hearing of their coming, gathered his men and went out to face them.

"Half of his men came back from the battle, but the other half remained on the field, and among the dead was Don Pedro himself. His death turned the people of San Triste into sheep. They could not think. They had not the strength to lift their hands. They stood about in little groups, whispering and muttering: 'They have murdered the Vereal!'

"But they had hardly time to say these things before the revolutionists came raving and ravaging into the town. They were wild for blood, and they got it. First of all they ran amuck through San Triste. Then they ran up the hill toward the Casa Vereal, swearing that they would slaughter every-body who wore that name.

"They spilled into the patio. I remember that half a dozen honest fellows tried to hold them at the gates for an instant. But their heads were dashed in with gun butts at once, or else they were chopped to the chin by machete strokes. When I saw that butchery, I knew that they would not stop until they had slaughtered every man in the house. I thought first of my treasure, and next of my own life, and last I remembered the little ten-year-old son of Don Pedro. I knew that the seconds were very precious if I wished to save my own life.

"I wished to fly to the treasure room at once, but first I could not help starting to hunt for little José. I found him with his French tutor, Louis Gaspard. Gaspard was an old man with long white hair and very polite manners; he was hardly bigger than little José, and he walked with a cane like a man who was about to fall into a grave.

"But when I saw him this day, he had forgotten his cane, he had straightened his bent back, and he was running with José in his arms, and the long white hair blowing out behind his head. What a picture that was! The dogs had wounded José with a chance shot through one of the windows. His head was streaming crimson, but he was as brave and as quiet as any man.

"'Are you hurt badly, José?' I heard Louis ask as he ran.

"'It is a mere nothing,' said José in French. 'Let me down; I can run for myself.'

"'He is cared for, then,' said I to myself. 'He is cared for as well as any one can be cared for in such a devil's time as this! Now every man for himself!'

"Was I not right to conclude in that fashion, John Jones?"

The latter made no answer, beyond a leisurely shrug of his shoulders.

"I flew down the passages and into the treasure room. There I waited for their coming, and I took a melancholy joy in the knowledge that I should die with all of my fortune scattered around me. But they did not come. In fact, I waited a whole day, and they did not come. Then I determined that, since I had not been found, I should try to make my escape. I

took a handful of the jewels. I stole up and found that the
house had been half wrecked by the soldiers of the revolution;
but there was now not a man living in it. I ventured out into
San Triste.

"All was quiet there. The revolutionists had marched on,
having done what harm they could. All was quiet, I say, until
I was seen, and then a yell went up like wolves when they see
a kill in sight, and food in the heart of the hungry winter. My
blood is still cold when I remember the wild face of the first
man who saw me. He ran at me like a madman. I shot him
down like one and fled for my life.

"For ten days they followed me. Nothing saved me except
that I had under me one of the finest of the horses of the
Vereal. I rode that horse to death before the end, but the men
of San Triste did not get me. They would have burned me to
death, inch by inch.

"The reason was partly because I had been a stern master
while I was among them in the place of the Vereal, and partly
because they had a stupid notion—God alone knows how it
came into their minds—that it was I who had brought down
the revolutionists upon the town of San Triste and that I had
done it because I wished to destroy the people because I could
no longer torment them.

"However this may be, at last I rode across the border and
was safe in the States again. I was about to start legal
proceedings when it came to me, suddenly, that I had no
proof that the money gathered in that treasure chamber
beneath the house was really my possession.

"If I laid a claim upon it, it would probably be confiscated
at once, for there were people in San Triste who would swear
that I was the earthly incarnation of the devil; they would
accuse me of being a revolutionist—anything to secure the
confiscation of my property.

"If it had been a small quantity of paper money, I could
have ventured back myself or else hired a thief to steal it for
me. But this treasure amounted to seventy mule loads. Such a
thing could not be spirited away in secret. As for my legal
claims upon the treasure, therefore, I could not put them
forward—I dared not reveal the presence of the secret chamber.

Theft was also impossible. For a year I brooded on the problem and nearly lost my mind struggling for a solution.

"At length I reconciled myself to a long delay. I turned the handful of jewels into cash. I went into business in New York and I found a new prosperity, though of course on a smaller scale. I gathered all the information I could concerning affairs in San Triste and I learned that the Cabrillos, as the nearest relatives of the Vereals, had claimed and taken the property unchallenged.

"As the years went on, I began to give up all hope, but eventually I heard of a strange rumor which was abroad in San Triste. It seems that, after the butchery, the bodies of little José and his tutor were not found among the killed. Several things might have happened. They might have been drowned in attempting to fly across the river, or else they might have been burned in the conflagration which consumed some of the outbuildings at the time of the masacre. Or else they might have fled, though in the last case it was strange that Louis Gaspard, when matters were again peacefully settled in San Triste, had not returned to reinstate his young master and claim his reward for faithfulness.

"However, it was held by some that, having carried José away to a good distance, the old man might have died, and José might have wandered away into a strange country—that his strange story of being a Vereal might not be believed— that perhaps, being only a child, he had never known that the revolution had blown over, and that his estate was waiting for his return. At any rate, there grew up a sort of legend in San Triste, that one day young José would come back to take up his patrimony and that the golden age would begin again for San Triste!

"Now, John Jones, I come to my great idea. I shall tell you what I did. I gathered together a dozen photographs of all the old Vereals. I had a composite photograph made. Then, from this and from the dozen pictures themselves, I had a painter paint the type as a sort of imaginary portrait. The result was this picture which you have seen."

He drew out the photograph of the oil painting.

"Next I hired three men, famous as adventurers, who were

willing to work beyond the law. I sent them out to find a man who closely resembled this picture. That is how, you see, I have met you.''

"I guessed that some time ago," said John Jones. "But now what is the plan?"

"It is beautifully simple, and wonderfully dangerous. You have recognized the resemblance between you and the picture, here. It is by no means a perfect likeness. Rather, it is a singular type which appears in both faces. But I think that it is enough, take it all in all, to make a sensation in San Triste.''

"I am to go there, in short, and claim the name of Vereal. I am to say that I am the lost Vereal?"

"Not so fast. Not half so fast, my friend. There are many details which must be explained to you."

"Suppose," said John Jones, "that knowing all of these things as you tell them to me, I ride down to San Triste and present my claims? I could take everything—and forget you?"

"No. I could betray you if you betrayed me.''

"But a bullet would put you out of the way, here and now.''

Simon stared at his youthful companion in a frozen ecstasy of terror and horror.

"Dear God!" he breathed at last. "You are a strange fellow, John Jones. But a bullet would not end me. If I disappear, within five days a letter of mine which is left in New York will be opened by a friend, and the instant that is done, the whole story will be revealed. When that story is known in San Triste, they will burn you to death.''

"I admit that you are not a fool," said John Jones calmly. "I am to go there alone, then, and having taken the property, I am to find a way of conveying the hidden money to you?"

"That will not be your work alone. I have already secured three capable assistants who will join you in San Triste and help in the work. It will be a problem big enough to occupy four brains. But your share is only to take and occupy the house and the other possessions of the Vereals. When you have done that, you may sit in quiet, simply allowing my three agents all liberty to work out a means of transporting the treasure to me, either piecemeal or in the bulk.''

"And my reward?"

"Whatever cash you wish, but first of all, you will be playing to win the entire huge Vereal estate. Truly, John Jones, you should speak of rewarding me for giving you such an opportunity."

"But suppose that they discover I am a pretender?"

"Then, beyond a shadow of a doubt, the people in San Triste would tear you to pieces, because in their eyes you would be guilty of a crime which is also almost a sacrilege."

9

If the people of San Triste had been asked what one act in all the history of the family of Vereal most nearly approached crime and folly in one, they would have pointed out, without the slightest hesitation, a single mésalliance. There were circumstances which made it unfortunate even at the time; the after-results were most terrible, they felt.

On a time the family of Vereal had been flourishing as much in numbers as in wealth and power, but in the process of the centuries the old line had been pinched thinner and thinner until at the last all the members could be counted upon the fingers of one hand and the births of male boys were hailed with the most frantic joy by the inhabitants of the town.

When this condition prevailed, the marriages of the daughters of the house were matters to be most seriously considered, since it was possible that such a marriage might mean the transfer, eventually, of the name and the possessions of the old family.

Of all the Vereals, it might have been expected that old Don Diego would have most carefully upheld the sacred traditions; but Don Diego himself was guilty of forming this mésalliance. His eldest child was a girl, and he had married her at an early age to a Cabrillo. The Cabrillos were manufacturers of pulque in the City of Mexico; worse than that, they were new even as manufacturers of liquor.

It was said that the old Cabrillo who started the family fortunes on the upgrade had been a common peon. At least, it was certain that the men and the women showed a common origin in their blunt-featured faces, all saving one, young Francisco. He was, in his youth, slenderly and actively made, gallant in manners and gay in his air.

In this fashion he came to the notice of Don Diego. They became friends; they became even intimates; and then, at the last, Vereal betrothed to this man his only daughter.

This he did, indeed, before he had so much as seen the family of his young friend. Those relatives, in fact, were carefully kept away from San Triste by young Francisco, but on the marriage day, when they came to witness the solemnities, and when the Vereal saw the types of the race—short nosed, small eyed, wide lipped—he had shuddered with repulsion. But the matter had gone too far. It could not be stopped. His daughter was married to a Cabrillo, and by that marriage there was a single son, Manuel.

Whatever his heart may have been, in appearance he was a true Cabrillo. He had short, bandy legs, a huge torso, long, powerful arms, a great thick neck worthy of a prizefighter, and upon his neck was placed a huge head with a low brow and outjutting jaws. He had received, in due course, an education in France and all the polish which careful tutors could give him, but howsoever his mind might reflect these labors, his exterior could not be reformed. He looked something like a great ape, and he acted the part very well, at times.

He it was who inherited all the great fortune of the Vereals, made stronger and richer than ever by the activity of Joseph Simon. He was sitting, on this day, under the palms which fringed the brow of the hill on which the Casa Vereal stood.

Opposite him was Federico de Alvarado who, now that the line of Vereal was extinguished in the town, represented its oldest and most honored family.

He was of a type quite opposite of Cabrillo. He was a very erect and sparely made gentleman of middle age, thin cheeked, somber eyed.

Cabrillo sat on the base of his spine, slouched forward, with his legs spraddling. Federico de Alvarado found him so repulsive that he could not look at him. They had been talking about small things, but Cabrillo was one who hated gradual advances. He liked to be in the heart of a discussion at a single stride. Now he raised his big voice, and a white-garbed mozo, a glimmering form behind the screen of the bushes where he waited, started forward.

"Bring tequila," said Cabrillo. "These wines are water. They fill the belly without satisfying it. Tequila, quick!"

At this, he grew suddenly so impatient with his desire that he leaped from his chair and walked hurriedly back and forth with his peculiar waddling gait until the new bottle was brought. He could not wait for the lemon to be squeezed; he snatched a glass, splashed it full of the colorless liquid, and then tossed off the drink.

After that he dropped into a chair, breathing heavily, his eyes half closed as he enjoyed the inward fire of that most potent liquor. Chuckling deep in his throat, he turned to the constrained face of his companion.

"Now, amígo, mio," said Cabrillo heartily, "I can talk. If God had not given us liquor, I should be a mute, or little better. But I can talk now. I have brought you here, in a word, because I wish that we may become the best of good friends, Alvaredo!"

The latter bowed and waved a graceful acceptance of this compliment. Then he looked hastily away. His glance traveled down sweeps of terraced lawns to great cypress trees which rose beside the Rio Sabrina, west and north, half encircling the house and its grounds. Someone was rowing down the Sabrina, and Alvarado followed the lazy swing and glitter of the oars with fascinated eyes. As a matter of fact, he was growing sick with apprehension, for he guessed what was to come.

"In one word," said Cabrillo, "I have read your letter concerning the money. If you cannot meet the interest this month, that is well enough. You shall not have to worry about it. In fact, as I pondered upon it, it seemed to me that we could very easily make an arrangement by which you would not owe me a single peso!"

Federico de Alvarado bit his thin lip, but he was forced to turn to his host and show some signs of surprise.

"How," said he, "can that possibly be, señor?"

"In this way. Look upon me, señor. Is there, you will say, anything that this man lacks? He is forty years of age, in the prime of a strong life; he has a great fortune in his control; he is housed better, I dare almost say, than any man in Mexico, and there is nothing left for him to desire. You will say this, but you will say wrong! There is one matter which I have overlooked.

"I had well nigh forgotten about it, but the other day I saw a woman's face, and suddenly I remembered that I was not married. That I must marry—beget children. Thought I to myself: 'Ten thousand devils! What if I should die without an heir and this great fortune pass to my pig of a cousin?' Now, señor, what do you say to that?"

"Why," said Alvarado slowly, "marriage is well enough, in its own place. But sometimes I am tempted to think that too many men marry because it is merely a custom."

"True, true," said Cabrillo heartily. "I despise—I hate such fellows. Beasts, I call 'em, señor. Let no man marry until he can no longer avoid it. Then when he sees a woman who puts a torch to his heart, he will know that he is in love. Let him wait for that time and then marry that woman!"

There was a little silence, during which Alvarado stirred uncomfortably in his chair.

"Perhaps," he said, "that may be the best way. Ah, what is that?"

There was a rapid beating of horses' hoofs. Then, on the river road, passing out from the town, they saw six rurales riding at a sharp trot, sweeping away with great speed.

"Ha!" cried Cabrillo, clapping his hands together and forgetting the subject of his conversation altogether, for the moment. "There will be news before morning. They will come back with their hands full. The devils! See how they ride! Straight in the saddle—all day they keep it up—that trot which will break the bones of other men—but they are not men—devils—wonderful devils! Where will you find, my friend, in any other land saving in Mexico, so many of such men?"

"Perhaps in no other," agreed Alvarado, delighted that the talk had turned to such a new theme. "There are no other men on earth to be matched with these rurales. How many of the gang of Grenacho did they run down last week?"

"Seven dead and three captured alive," said Cabrillo. "However, not one of the three will talk. They have more dread of Grenacho a hundred miles away than they have of a hundred rurales at their elbows! Ah, there is a man! But I shall have him yet—and grind him—so—under my heel—the dog!"

In a sudden transport of anger, he dropped his glass to the ground and stamped it to slivers.

"Why do you hate him more than others?" asked Alvarado in his quiet voice.

"I had rather cut out my tongue than name him. But to you, it is different, I hope. You have not heard, then, what Grenacho said when he was asked why he broke his oath and was again robbing and killing in the district of San Triste?"

"I have not heard that."

"His answer was this: I gave my oath to a man and a family of men! There is no longer a Vereal. You have let a pig sit down in the place of a man. Now you must suffer for it.' "

Cabrillo groaned with fury. "That was his word for me—a pig in the place of a man. But I shall have him yet!"

Here Alvarado was seized by a little fit of coughing which made him cover his face with his hand. When he looked up again, his eyes were bright with moisture.

"Yet," he said, "one cannot waste emotion on the speeches of a bandit, my friend Cabrillo."

"For you, perhaps not. For me, it is otherwise. So! So!"

He expelled his breath in great gasps until his little bright eyes ceased to roll. Then he said suddenly: "But there is the other matter which is of more importance than this dog, this Grenacho. It is the marriage with your daughter! Yes, yes, señor. You start, but it is she whom I have chosen. The beautiful Alicia!"

"She," said Alvarado huskily, "is hardly better than a child."

"Bah! She is eighteen. They should all be married by that age. Marriage will keep them from mischief. They are too much for a father. They need the bit and the bridle and the spurs. They need a husband to control 'em."

Alvarado had grown pale. "Señor," he said, bowing again, "you cover me with obligations. This is a matter, however, which must be thought upon. I cannot answer offhand—"

"No?" said Cabrillo, with a ring of anger in his voice. "Do such suitors as Cabrillo come every day, then, to tap at your door?"

Alvarado set his teeth over a retort which had stormed into his throat almost before he could control it.

"I confess that you honor me greatly, and my daughter," said he. "But of course, her mother must be consulted in this matter. You will agree to that?"

"I speak plain business," said Cabrillo, slapping his big hand upon the little table until the glasses danced and jiggled. "This is what I tell you: In the name of business, you owe me money, and I must be paid. But I am liberal. You may pay me with cash, or else you may pay me in another fashion with your daughter. You see, I am frank. In your affairs, you have been foolish. But God has given you a treasure. Part with it, and you will need to worry no more about finance. I, Cabrillo, pledge my word to you for that!"

Alvarado rose. "I go at once," he said in a stifled voice, "to speak to my wife. Señor, my gratitude to you; I beg you to have patience!"

He departed in this fashion. Seated in his carriage in the courtyard, he said to the coachman: "The whip, Juan, the whip! I must be at home in the twinkling of an eye!"

So the carriage thundered out of the yard and down the hill

into San Triste. He hurried into his house and found his wife in the patio garden.

"My dear," said Alvarado, drawing her to the side, "we are ruined; the worst has come. The brute on the hill in La Casa Vereal will either have full payment or our daughter!"

The señora grew stiff as a statue, and her thin lips compressed. But she thought before she spoke, and finally her eyes twinkled.

"After all," she said, "there are times when pride must be put in the pocket. All things must be considered. If Cabrillo is a pig, as you say, at least his house is not a sty!"

10

When John Jones, alias the Kid, first caught sight of San Triste, it was a ghost city of purest white and so clearly cut that he could have numbered the houses, one by one, and mapped every street.

After the heat of the day, it was a dream of perfect coolness and perfect rest, and John Jones drew rein among the wilderness of thorny brush through which he was riding to enjoy the scene. He had studied through many careful hours the map with which Joseph Simon had provided him, and now he could pick out the details and name them, one by one—the dark bushing of trees which was the Plaza Municipal, the Rio Sabrina, twisting down in leisurely fashion until its waters spread into the quiet of a lagoon, the meadows between the river and the town, the ruins of the smelters on the northern side of the Sabrina, the cane fields beyond, and far to the north and west the strong blue forms of the mountains.

He picked them out one by one, gave them their names, and assured himself that the memory of Joseph Simon had been of a photographic exactness. Then he let the black horse jog down into the hollow from which his view was quite shut off from the town. Here was a rude wakening from his schemes, for two ragged fellows started up before him and covered him with leveled rifles.

They ordered his hands up with a stream of oaths, but John Jones merely folded one hand upon the other and rested them on the top of the pommel of his saddle.

"Who has sent you on this fool's errand?" asked John Jones in his quiet voice.

"Tell him, Juan," said one of the two, "for it will save us a bullet."

"Grenacho!" cried Juan, and then both grinned behind their guns, as though they expected the sound of that dreadful name to tumble their victim out of his saddle. John Jones, however, merely smiled and shook his head. When they yelled at him to put up his hands, he merely raised one with a mildly commanding gesture.

"My children," said he, "can you look at me and fail to understand?"

Their savage grins were wiped away; they began to stare at him with wonder. Of late, the name of Grenacho had been like the yell of a wolf among sheep to the people of the district of San Triste. To be so quietly encountered by this man who did not even touch a gun but merely smiled down at them, bewildered the simple minds of the bandits.

"Look again—look closer!" commanded John Jones, and he sent the black horse a step or two nearer to them. They shrank away from him, and then tightened the grip of their uncertain hands upon their weapons.

"Who is it? What is it?" he heard one whisper to the other.

"The devil, perhaps. I don't know!" murmured the other. He raised his voice: "Stand quiet or I shoot, señor!"

"You may be my messengers," replied the rider as calmly as ever. "Go to Grenacho and tell him that the oath which he swore to the Vereal is once more binding, for the Vereal has returned, and I am he. José Vereal has returned. Tell him that if he dares to lay hands again upon a man of San Triste, I shall myself ride into the mountains and find him, and burn him out of his hole. As for you, I forgive you, as being fools. Adios!''

How much they believed him, he could not tell, but above all he did not wish to stay and to argue. He pressed a knee against the ribs of the black stallion and passed deliberately forward between the muzzles of the rifles, felt them swing in to cover him from the rear, and set his teeth in expectation of receiving a volley from behind.

But not a word was spoken, nor was a trigger touched, while he passed slowly up the slope and then dipped across the brow of the next low hill. When he was out of sight, he heard a loud sort of wailing cry from the two behind him. Whether they had been wakened from their trance of astonishment and fallen into a fury at the thought of an escaped prey, he could not tell, but still he would not hurry his pace, and neither of the pair appeared again during the rest of his ride to the town.

His spirits began to rise at every step and his self-confidence increased tenfold, for he said to himself that the first blow in the battle had been struck by him and after that, all would be much simpler. Having announced himself, he could fit into his part with a far greater ease.

He was in no hurry, however, to enter the town, but swinging now to the left, he began to obtain from the meadowland near the lagoon a clear view of that northern hill near the river on top of which stood the Casa Vereal. Its long walls, visible behind the screening masses of trees, seemed to enclose ground enough for a palace.

What he must do next, he could not decide. Somewhere in the town of San Triste, according to the plan, were Halsey and Denny and Marmont, ready to fall in behind him so soon as he showed himself and made a move. But what that move was to be, not even the clever brain of Joseph Simon had been able to devise.

''You are my general, John Jones,'' he had said to the latter, almost at the moment of farewell. ''I have planned the whole campaign, but after I get you to the field of battle, the rest must remain with you. You must decide where to charge and how!''

All this had seemed not impossible when he was far away, north of the Rio Grande, but now that he lingered in the late dusk near the lagoon and under the cypress trees, unreal in their immensity, he began to feel that he, a single man, was about to attempt to storm a whole city. It was worse than a forlorn hope; it was a feat of madness.

He decided, at the last, that he must slip away from his horse and reconnoiter the town, or part of it, secretly and on foot. So he threw the reins of the black stallion, removed the saddle, so that the weary animal could rest, and then strapped a blanket about its body. For here was no wild-headed, iron-limbed bronco. The black horse was made like a picture, slender limbed, but with great power of shoulders and haunches to whip those delicate legs over the ground.

He had traveled fast and far on this day, but still nothing could depress that dauntless head or take the fire out of his eye. He began to crop the grasses quietly so long as his master was nearby, but when John Jones turned away, the black stallion began to dance and whinny softly in anxiety. John Jones came quickly back. He was touched as he had rarely been touched before in all his life.

North of the Rio Grande, the very air he breathed was friendly and familiar, the mountains were known to him, and the towns and the people; but in this southland the very ways of the rivers seemed unusual, and the white city of San Triste, now turning to blue and gray in the night, was a place of unknown peril. The black horse became more than a horse; it became a companion in a time of peril, and passing an arm around the neck of the animal, he stood there a moment with his head bowed beside the head of the horse, thinking. The horse was quiet as stone, also.

When John Jones went away again, the black did not whinny or dance; it merely lifted its fine head and pricked its ears, as though in that interval of silence it had received a message and had understood.

If, at that moment, John Jones had been offered the life and the soul of the greatest and the richest human being on the earth in exchange for the life of his black horse, Pierre, he would have laughed the thought to scorn. The horse was a friend who would never fail him.

Certainly it was a grave young man, with two-thirds of his gaiety cast behind him, who walked slowly up from the meadows and toward the town. He said to himself that he had, however, three allies, quite aside from the three men who were waiting for him in the town. They were factors, but they would only become effective after he had himself taken the bull by the horns.

His three friends, therefore, were only the black stallion by the lagoon, which would secure his retreat if he could run to it; the second was a long knife, sharper than a razor, and terrible beyond words in the grip of Jones; the third friend, whose voice was the loudest of the three, was a long and heavy Colt revolver.

He flicked the weapon from its holster and passed it with an incredible lightness over the tips of his fingers. By those delicate tips he could read it and recognize it as another might know a familiar face with his eyes. Every worn place and every small notch meant something to John Jones. When he put the gun away again, his courage had been raised to the highest point, and he was ready to begin his adventure.

11

When John Jones came to the edge of the town, he was prepared to go forward with most careful stealth, but he found that there was already in progress a disturbance which would amply cover his approach. It was, in fact, ridiculously easy to spy upon the town of San Triste on this night.

It seemed to John Jones that, far and wide through the

town, he could hear a murmur passing; it grew thick and audible in the nearest street, and finally out of the noise a single name started and made his heart leap. Men had uttered it thickly. But now a woman's voice shrilled it above the crowd's voices: "El Vereal!"

That was the cause of the trouble, then. The Vereal! The two bandits had made announcement of his coming!

He bit his lips with vexation. He had used that magic name with the two robbers simply as a means of extricating himself from a grave difficulty. How could he dream that two renegades such as these could dare to come into the heart of a town like San Triste, where each of them must be wanted a dozen times by the law, and there venture to relate one of their holdup attempts and its strange outcome?

However, the damage was done. He had hoped that he could linger about the town for some days, learning more of its people, getting in touch with his three confederates, and waiting for an opportunity to strike with some advantage after he had consulted with them. But all the hopes which were built upon such thoughts were now brushed away. He must act at once to take advantage, if indeed there was an advantage in it, of the sudden name and influence of the Vereal upon the townsfolk.

But ten years had passed—or was it a round dozen?—since a Vereal had lived in that town. Who would remember the features of the family well enough to see in his own at least a general resemblance to the old type of the Vereal? What would that recognition mean to the town? What was their attitude toward Cabrillo? That was another item about which Simon had not been sure.

He approached the street with some confidence, certain that the growing uproar would cover him. Finally he secured a post of vantage in a clump of shrubbery between two dobe houses.

He found a general tumult surpassing his expectations. The whole street was astir with women with black shawls drawn over their heads, or with the darting bodies of half-naked children or ragged peons. There was no central point, however, around which the scene grouped. He only heard murmurs and chance phrases, and the expressions of the faces, it seemed to John Jones, indicated fear rather than any other emotion.

Suddenly the little mob resolved itself into a more or less ordered audience. Someone was coming with definite information, so it seemed. He was conducted down the street by a prosperous-looking fellow who swelled with his own importance in bringing such a herald. Now he paused, raised both hands, and with a few shouted words gathered the whole flock about him. They were ranged in a dense circle. All faces were turned inward, watching him intently.

"Pedro," said the man of importance, "has the whole story. He will tell us. Let us be silent and consider well what he says. This is a strange night for San Triste. This is a night which we will all remember until we are old. Speak, Pedro!"

Pedro was a gloomy, sullen man, depressed by abject poverty. His clothes were rags; his face had the scarred look of the laborer. However, the most miserable of the wretched, south of the Rio Grande, can tell a tale, and now the haggard face of Pedro lighted with the fiery inspiration of the narrator.

"I tell you the story word for word as I have just heard it," said Pedro. "God has put his hand on me now—now—if I change one word of it!" Solemnly, he crossed himself.

It was like the taking of the oath in a court of law, and John Jones, tensed and excited as he was, could not help smiling to himself. The crowd began to listen with a religious intensity.

"It happened in this fashion," began the teller of the tale. "Juan Oñate and Gomez, the baker, were walking through the brush, coming over the hills from the south. They had stopped on the top of a hill and looked all around them, as tired men will do, friends, when they see there is still a distance to go and they see their homes and they wish that they were there."

The crowd nodded. These circumstantial details gave foundation for whatever was to come.

"While they stayed there, they began to talk," went on Pedro. "They talked a little of the old days. They talked of a time when Oñate worked in the house of the Vereal."

Here he made a pause, and a little shiver, so it seemed, ran through the crowd and a murmur: "El Vereal!"

"You, Cabeza," said Pedro, "would remember when Oñate
worked there!"

The prosperous fellow who had brought the talebearer now
cleared his throat and nodded. "I remember very well," he
said. "I remember one day I was teaching young Don
José—God rest him—"

The crowd murmured softly, with a sound like a wave
drawing off a shore: "God rest him!"

"I was teaching young Don José how to handle his spurs.
He handled them! Ha, ha, ha! He handled them so well that
he brought the blood from the mare he was riding. She grew
wild and tossed him over her head. I thought he was killed. I
ran to him with a cry, but he jumped up laughing—he jumped
up laughing, for that was the Vereal."

There was a hoarse muttering of assent from the crowd.

"He said to me: 'I cannot help that throw. I shall ride the
mare again. But send away that man with the fat face. It
makes me laugh to see him. I cannot ride while I laugh!'"

The crowd laughed heartily, but briefly, eager to be at the
rest of the story.

"Well," said Cabeza, "that man with the fat face was
Oñate. Yes, I remember very well. Go on, Pedro. What of
Oñate?"

"Oñate talked of the old days in La Casa Vereal," said
Pedro. He said, 'There will never be happy days for San
Triste again until a Vereal is master in the house on the
hill.'"

John Jones listened with all his heart, and his blood leaped
at the almost stern muttering of assent.

"With that," said Pedro, "they had turned to go on their
way, when they heard a horse trampling behind them. They
turned in surprise, because there had been no horse within a
mile of them the last time they looked behind. But now they
saw a great black horse come down into the hollow where
they were, and on the back of the black horse there was a
young man, handsome, gay, rich. His face was the face of
young Don José grown into a man!"

At this all restraint was swept from the crowd. They raised

their voices in a hoarse shout that roared in the ears of John Jones.

"They were made dumb by such a thing. It could not be true. They told one another with their eyes that this was a terrible ghost come to haunt them. What will you say, friends, were the first words of the man—or the ghost?" The crowd grew in its breath with a hissing sound and waited, trembling.

"The first words were: 'My children, I have—' "

What a groan of sorrow and of joy from these huddled people! Men and women looked at one another through eyes bright with tears.

"He said," went on Pedro, " 'My children, I have heard of your unhappiness while a stranger lives in the house on the hill. But have no fear. I have come again to comfort you. I am here, and I have come to stay among you and to keep watch over you as my fathers have done before me!'

"At that they dropped upon their knees, Oñate and Gomez, and tried to cry out to him and bless him, but they found that their voices, by a miracle, had been stopped in their throats. They tried with all their might to bless him, I say, and they could not speak. Tears ran into their eyes. God knows, friends, that had I been there, I should have not been able to see my own hands because of weeping. But when they could look again, the Vereal was gone from before them!"

There was a deep groan of dismay from the throng, and cries: "No, no! He would not have gone, after he had come to be our comfort."

"Hush! Hush!" cried Pedro harshly. "God be my judge that you are fools to dream that you are fit to speak a word upon the Vereal and what he would do. He vanished, or the dream that wore his shape vanished. But a token was left behind him. I tell you, friends, that when Oñate and Gomez looked down upon the ground before them, each of them found that a gold coin had been tossed there. They picked them up and blessed themselves that it was the truth and not a dream which they had seen.

"Then they looked closely at the coins. What will you say when you know? The dates upon the coins were the same, and upon each was a date of a dozen years before! What happened in that year? In that year, friends, alas, in that year we betrayed the Vereal and let him be butchered by dogs and let the same dogs rush at his house.''

A hoarse yell of anger and of resolution rose from the listeners.

John Jones waited to hear no more. There was a soft rustling in the brush where he was hiding. Then he had slipped away and was running through the night swiftly, with a step as long and as light as the stride of an Indian runner. Down to the lagoon—now shimmering in a dull mist of moonshine—he hastened.

Upon the back of Pierre, who whinnied an eager welcome, he threw the saddle. Into the saddle he flung himself, and up the slope toward San Triste he took his way. He had nothing but impulse to guide him, but he felt that in this moment impulse was a stronger and a better guide than much reason.

12

On the very verge of the town he paused and made his last preparations. From his clothes he dusted the dirt of the journey as well as he could, and then he added the touches which Joseph Simon had advised. From a saddlebag he took out a black cloak and shook the folds from it. This he draped over his shoulders. Around his wrist he tied a scarf of great length and of the most brilliant red and gold.

Then, furling up one side of his sombrero and sending Pierre into a state of prancing ecstasy with a touch of his heel and a slight check upon the rein, he danced into that street of San Triste where the first chapter of his strange new life was to be written.

No one saw him at the first. The crowd was still held

around Pedro in the center of the place. He was repeating his
story in undying vigor for the fifth time. He was embroidering
little details as fast as they were asked for, when a wild cry
from one in the rear of his circle cut his story short. It was a
cry like the voice of a ghost in the middle of a ghost story.

"El Vereal!"

They turned, stricken with shuddering terror and with
amazement. There they saw a gallant figure upon a shining
black stallion which pranced across the shaft of light cast out
through the open door of one of the huts.

At that first cry the heart of John Jones stopped. It did not
beat, he could have sworn, while the great black stallion went
so gaily through the second shaft of light that washed out
from the doorway into the street, dim and flickering, but
bright enough to show the black horse—bright enough to
show the colors of the house of Vereal knotted at the waist of
the stranger.

But not a whisper's volume of sound had come from the
crowd since the first shout. Not so much as a gasp or a groan
was heard until, coming still closer, the people saw the
aquiline, handsome face of the rider who approached them,
the dark cloak blowing from his shoulders, the grace and the
dignity of his posture in the saddle; and then the voice rose as
from one throat—the giant throat of a crowd, rejoicing, glad
to the point of sorrow: "El Vereal!"

They ran for him—the women with their arms extended as
though to welcome a returned son to their family, the men
shaking their fists and their hats in the air. They rushed at him
as though they would sweep even the big stallion from its
feet, but at the last moment they split away before him as
though his nearer presence were a wall of stone which held
them back. They split away, they swarmed into a tangle all
around him. What a wailing cry of joy thrilled in the ears of
John Jones!

But what that gay young man was saying to himself was:
"I am a villain! I am ten times a villain to deceive them!
They are cheering for El Vereal, and I am a hired imposter!"

Such was the thought of John Jones. But who could resist

playing a part on such a stage, so set, and with the speeches written out for him by his very audience?

He raised a hand, and they were hushed like school children before a stern master.

"My children—" began John Jones.

He could not say more. They drowned his voice with their sudden uproar. Suddenly he stretched out his hand. They were stilled again.

"Cabeza!" he said. "You have not forgotten me? You remember the mare—and the fall?"

Perhaps there had been some who kept a doubt in their heart of hearts, but all this positive proof that all was well, the last doubt was washed away. Not a man or a woman or a child but would have staked his life that this was the veritable heir to La Casa Vereal on the hill above San Triste—not one but would have laid down his life to replace him where they felt he belonged.

As for Cabeza, the crowd was very thick just before him, but he burst through it as though it were no more than so many paper images. For he was a big man, and the years had hardened his strength instead of turning his muscles to fat. He took the outstretched hand of the Vereal in both of his, and the tears flowed down his face. His throat was choked. He could not speak until at last a sort of groaning sigh burst from him.

"Oh, my dear master! God has forgiven my sins by sending you back to San Triste. I have seen Don José again; now let me die!"

John Jones drew him closer and leaned from the saddle.

"Cabeza," he said, "if God has sent me back to San Triste, San Triste will be happy to have me. But there is one man in this city who may be a trifle sad when he hears that I have come at last."

With this he raised his hand and pointed above the heads of the crowd and toward the cluster of trees which shrouded the Casa Vereal upon the top of the northern hill.

Cabeza nodded grimly. "He has sent word to the police. The gendarmes have their orders. You are to be arrested, dear master, as soon as you show your face in the city. Perhaps even at this moment the gendarmes are hurrying to this place.''

He cast over his shoulder, as he spoke, a troubled glance toward the upper end of the street where it passed on toward the heart of the city.

Then, turning to John Jones again: "What shall be done? If one life will aid you, it is yours, God knows!"

"There shall be no shedding of blood," said the rider calmly. "But are there no horses here? I must have people on horseback behind me. If there are guns in the holsters—perhaps the gendarmes will change their minds, perhaps they will postpone an arrest?"

A smile flickered upon the lips of Cabeza. He turned away and raised a voice which bellowed and boomed above the crowd—a few broken exclamations, a few sharp, clear orders—and instantly every owner of a horse rushed to saddle it. Only the women and the children and the old men were left for a moment around the rider of the black horse, and they swarmed closer.

A woman lifted a thin-faced child to look more closely at the stranger, and the sickly infant screamed with terror. John Jones bit his lip. Then he summoned all his courage and took the child quickly in his arms. Terror, perhaps, choked it. It lay, quietly, staring up to him. There was a murmur of awe and of admiration from those crowding women. This, to them, was a miracle.

"The doctor," cried the anxious mother, "says that my baby must die. Tell me, oh, tell me, Don José, that he has lied to me!"

"I shall have that doctor whipped out of San Triste," said John Jones sternly. "The man is a fool. This child shall live. It must live. Take this"—and he put a rustling bill for ten pesos in her hand—"feed it well, keep the baby clean, trust in the good God, and you need not fear!"

"I shall trust in El Vereal!" sobbed the woman, trembling with joy. "And pray for you, señor, señor!"

She took the child and drew back into the crowd, cherishing it. Recovering from the fear that had checked its outcries, it began to whimper again.

"Look! Look!" cried the excited mother. "It cries to go back to the arms of El Vereal!"

Let cold-hearted men say and think what they pleased, the women of San Triste had seen a very real, very convincing miracle. The men had seen, so they thought, the face of El Vereal come back to them. But the women were ready to swear that they had seen the warm heart of the Vereal.

So it was that when the men were ready to ride with this false Don José, the women were ready to march with their husbands and their sons and their fathers; and as all the world knows, a mob of women is more terrible than a drilled army of fighting soldiers.

In the meantime, thirty men were mounted. It was a small group, and as John Jones looked back upon them, his own heart somewhat misgave him. Certainly he had not chosen of the fattest or the most populous quarter of San Triste in which to make his first appearance. They were beggared workmen, one and all, with the sole exception of Cabeza himself, who was the rich man of the quarter. But even his horse was simply an ugly-headed mustang, and the mounts of the others were indescribable racks of bones.

What better could be expected? The men of San Triste, having hardly enough to link their own bodies firmly to their souls, could hardly waste precious money in providing ample nutriment for their horses.

Upon these shambling skeletons, however, the thirty men who were mounted were bold, lusty fellows. So far as courage and devotion to a cause would go, they could not be surpassed, but, unfortunately, they had few firearms. Bullets cost money.

Their arms consisted of knives, and above all, the sharp, heavy machetes with which they worked in the cane fields and with which they were willing to work on this day at human flesh and bone, if the cause demanded such efforts. However, what would less than twoscore sword arms accomplish against three or four repeating rifles?

John Jones looked again to the house on the hill, squat and huge behind the veiling masses of the trees. To storm such a fortress with such a handful was a madness beyond even his

wild conceptions. They must work in another way. They had
started by miracles, and it was by miracles alone that he
could continue. That thought appealed to him strongly, and he
suppressed what would have been the broadest of grins.

Cabeza had now marshaled his men in a sort of clumsy
colunm, with women and children tangled on its flanks and
John Jones at its head. When Cabeza gave the word to march,
he was answered by a tremendous cheer, or rather a yell, in
which the shrill voices of the women and the children
overrode the deeper voices of the men.

"Viva El Vereal!"

13

It was the last thing that John Jones desired. That shout
announced to the enemy the exact location from which the
danger was formed and approaching, but it was impossible to
suppress the voices of that tiny army. From the moment the
march began the air was rent with one prolonged uproar. Five
thousand, it seemed, could hardly have made such a bulk of
noise. Through the confusion, Cabeza shouted at the ear of
the false Vereal.

"We have started, señor, but where now do we go?"

There was only one answer which came into the mind of
John Jones and he gave it: "To La Casa Vereal!"

That word was instantly repeated by his lieutenant, and the
crowd took it up: "To La Casa Vereal!"

They moved slowly, very slowly forward, according to the
pace of John Jones on his black charger, for he knew that if
this was the wave which was to roll over the big building on
the hill, it must gather much head before it arrived. Gather it
did, with the most amazing speed. The men stayed closer

together, shouting, cheering; the women were his recruiting agents. They ran here and there, everywhere before the little advancing troop. They entered houses and dragged the startled occupants out, or they caught by the arms men who had already run in amazement to discover the cause of the outcry.

Their enthusiasm was wildly contagious. In one second, with a few chattered words, a few crazed gestures, and the cry: "Vereal!" they could convince the most stolid citizen of San Triste that miracles were indeed in the air—that the dead had risen—that anything, in short, could be expected.

They caught up their weapons; those who had horses, saddled them and mounted in wild haste; and on the way they caught bits and fragments of information. They learned that the Vereal had come in person, handsome, young, gay, and brave, to claim what was his by the right of birth and to unseat that detested monster who held the house on the hill.

In a brief ten minutes the original thirty had been multiplied by ten, and the attending flocks of people began to choke up the street on either side. But still more and more were coming in, for John Jones was following a winding course, slowly, slowly, through the heart of the town, giving time to all who would come to him. All who came were not like other men—they were beings on fire, the fire of eagerness, and of romance.

One came before him, quivering, shuddering with excitement. "Señor, señor!" he cried, throwing out his arms. "Teach me how to die for you! Show me in what way—"

"Go up the hill," answered John Jones like a good general, "and find out for us what Cabrillo is doing."

The man wheeled and flogged and spurred his poor horse out of sight in a twinkling. Others followed that lead without waiting to be bidden. Such was the spirit of the men of San Triste. If there were any who doubted, they were seized and dragged instantly to the head of the column. "Look!" they were commanded. "Let your eyes tell you for yourself!"

One such glance was sufficient. Under such conditions black instantly would have been admitted to be the most perfect white.

There was a slight whirlpool formed in the mass of men

near him by the resolute advance of three horsemen, urging their mounts on in a close group, and one seconding the other. They came closer, and by the wild light of one of the torches which some of the men had kindled, John Jones saw his confederates: the Englishman, the American, the Frenchman.

They reached him presently, and Si Denny, driving close, cried under his breath: "Fine work, Kid. Fine work. You're doing 'em up brown!"

"But what if Cabrillo hits this crowd with twenty horsemen who'll fight together?"

"The four of us will make a stand, and the others will finish the job for us. Besides," went on Denny, surveying the terrible faces in the crowd, "these boys mean business. Rifles wouldn't stop 'em tonight. They're drunk with the sort of stuff that stays in the head, not the stomach!"

It was true, as John Jones could see for himself. They were men transformed.

The first scout came back to them on a horse staggering with weariness and struck into a lather by the cruel speed by its rider. Cabrillo had had the news long before, was the word which the scout carried. He had assembled with him in the house on the hill some scores of men, wholly dependent upon him, owing their prosperity or their privation wholly to his success or his failure.

For, finding himself thoroughly hated in the city itself, he had made haste to gather around him a precious crew of ruffians who pretended to run his farms near the town of San Triste, but who, in reality, merely sat back and enjoyed the incomes which the farms brought in. Such fellows as these would fight and fight to kill, and though their numbers might be small, they needed only good leaders in order to make a formidable showing. Cabrillo was just such a man as would take them into the thick of the fire.

What showing the mob of the Kid's half-armed followers could make against such men, the leader could not guess. But the mob itself, of course, had no doubt. What it wanted, almost as much as to replace this pretender in the house of his assumed ancestors, was to get hands upon Cabrillo, who had diverted the patronage of the Vereal estate to strangers, hirelings who were his bulwark by the strength of their hands and their weapons.

In the meantime, they had passed from the poorer section of that part of San Triste, and were entering a quarter where the streets, indeed, were no broader, but where the houses were of great size.

Marmont now pointed out one of the largest of these buildings. "There it is," he said. "There's the key to the rest of San Triste. You have the poor men. Now, you can get the rich ones to follow you like sheep if Alvarado will take the lead after you. He's the king since the Vereal disappeared. Get Alvarado and the trick is turned and finished."

So they came to the house of Alvarado, and the crowd, as though realizing fully and at once the importance of making this convert to their growing cause, set up a tremendous shouting upon Alvarado to come out to them. For some moments not so much as a light gleamed behind the few and narrow casements which looked out upon the street from the rear of the old aristocrat's mansion.

But presently a door opened and Alvarado himself stepped out onto a narrow balcony which extended just over the entrance arch which led into the interior court. A big mozo came behind him and held up a lantern as though to help his master view the crowd. As a matter of fact, that crowd was sufficiently illumined by the torches they carried, and the mozo's lantern merely served to cast a bright light upon the form of Alvarado himself.

The Kid viewed with concern that slender figure, the pride and the pallor of Alvarado's face. The latter raised a hand, and the clamoring in the street fell away at the signal.

"What is this?" asked Alvarado quietly. "Why have you come to me? Is some danger threatening San Triste?"

The answer was with the united roaring of a hundred voices: "The Vereal! The Vereal has come back to us!"

The Kid rode the black horse a little nearer to that impassive form on the balcony.

"Señor Alvarado," he said, "if you have forgotten me, I can blame the dozen years which have passed since I was last in San Triste. But now I have come back to reclaim what is mine. Will you ride with me, señor, to La Casa Vereal? I have proved to the men of the town that I am José Vereal."

Alvarado did not reply instantly. A dozen lights had been raised by willing hands in the mob to illumine for his inspection the face of the Kid, and while Alvarado surveyed him, his fingers drummed lightly upon the edge of the balcony railing.

He said at last in the same unemotional manner: "Señor Don José Vereal, since that is the name by which you call yourself, if you have a claim upon the property of the Vereal in San Triste, are there not courts and judges and juries in this city which will establish you inside your rights? But you have appealed to a crowd."

At this, the crowd muttered, but was instantly hushed to hear the rejoinder of the Kid.

He now said: "I can tell you my story in an instant. Louis Gaspard took me out of Mexico as fast as a train would whirl us along when we left San Triste on the night La Casa Vereal was stormed. We took a steamer from Vera Cruz to New Orleans, Louis Gaspard telling me all the time that I must never go back to San Triste.

"He died a few days after we reached the States. But though I was only a child of ten, señor, I could not forget San Triste. For the only air which does not choke a Vereal is the air of San Triste!"

There was a deafening shout from the gathering at this announcement, made in a ringing voice. But it seemed to the Kid that the man on the balcony sneered a little at this flower of rhetoric. The Kid bit his lip. He saw plainly that he could not talk to a crowd and to a single gentleman at one and the same time. What stirred the one made the other smile.

"So, after a dozen years," said Federico de Alvarado, "you have decided to return to us. I wish you joy of your return, Señor Vereal. So soon as the courts of law have given you their sanction, I shall ask you to number me among your most humble servants and permit me to call on you in La Casa Vereal to pay my respects."

A rumble of doubt, wonder, and disapproval came from the mass in the street. It began to sway and pitch. Then a sharp

voice, a harsh and biting voice, which the Kid knew came
from the throat of the Englishman, Halsey, cried: "Down
with Alvarado! He is in league with Cabrillo. He is fed by the
swine who lives in the house on the hill!"

It was very good Spanish which Halsey spoke, and he
roared it out with a vim. A mob is a horse which needs little
of the spur, but the crowd in that street of San Triste went
instantly mad. Here was a barrier in front of their newfound
hero. They did not only wish to wash over it; they wished to
smash it to bits. An instant before they had looked up into the
calm, sneering face of Alvarado as children toward a master,
but that lion's roar from Halsey changed them.

A keen pencil of light darted at Alvarado and clanged
against the dobe wall behind him, where it turned into a
heavy knife and dropped to the street. Other knives were out,
and revolvers and rifles were made ready. In another second
there would be a volley which would blow Alvarado limb
from limb.

In the face of this most deadly peril he was magnificent.
He merely folded his arms and leaned lightly against the frail
iron grill which skirted his balcony, and the smile of contempt
had not changed on his lips; rather than turn his back, it was
patent that he would die a dozen deaths.

The Kid cried out sharply; his voice was lost in the
ominous bellowing which now crowded the street with echoes
up and down and swelled more and more heavily. Besides,
here was Halsey, his plump face crimson with the delight of
mischief.

He gripped the arm of the Kid with the hand of a giant.
"Shut up!" he cautioned swiftly. "Let them go. Let Alvarado
go! Besides the rascal thinks too much and too well to suit us.
Let us have simple men, or none at all!"

To this cruelly ironical speech, the Kid did not listen at all.
He was still striving vainly to make himself heard, but vainly.
Then, as he pushed forward, a gun barked just beside his ear
and he saw the head of Alvarado flinch to one side from the
whiz of the bullet. Si Denny had decided that matters were
not progressing as fast as they should, and he was taking it
into his hand to speed things along. Indeed, not the half part

of a second would have remained for the stubborn fellow on the balcony had not he been saved almost against his will. The Kid saw a girl in a red dress flash through the door on to the balcony and slip in front of Alvarado. There, with her bare arms thrown wide as if to shelter him the more completely, she looked up to his face with such an agony of terror and love that the picture burned itself deep in the mind of the Kid.

It was the end of the peril of Alvarado. The Mexican loves courage only more than he cares for a stirring and beautiful spectacle. The guns were lowered; the knives were waved in the air; a thousand voices were shouting: "Viva la señorita!" Then the mass rolled on and drew the Kid with it.

He went gaily, with a sudden warmth of happiness which he could not understand, except that it sprang, he knew, from the knowledge that she was the daughter of Alvarado—not his wife! They passed other houses; more people came out to them. A few of the patrician class in San Triste held back as Alvarado had done, but the majority instantly joined the procession with an enthusiasm as wild and almost as noisy as that of the peons.

Young cavaliers and old darted their horses into the mob and came to wring his hand or to embrace him; tears shone in their eyes; shouts of joy were on their lips; and John Jones knew at last he had won San Triste and with it he had won La Casa Vereal and the great treasure which was buried in it.

14

They poured north, now. Half of San Triste had been drained dry of men, and the other half was sending in recruits at the gallop. There was no longer a chance that they might be effectively resisted by a handful of defenders at La Casa

Vereal. The Kid could be sure of that as his army streamed out of the northern verge of San Triste and began to climb the hill.

A hundred lights tossed and staggered above the heads of the long column which, thickly compacted at the head, straggled and spread behind like the flaring tail of a comet, and wherever John Jones looked he saw the same wild faces, the same deadly glint of naked steel.

Those fellows would never be needed, however, for the aristocracy of San Triste was gathered at the front, ranged closely around their leader. Here were some scores of gallant men admirably mounted, armed to the teeth with revolvers and rifles.

They introduced themselves, as though knowing that a dozen years must have blotted their names and faces from his memory. Old Antonio Mendoza rode before him, swearing that to reach his beloved Vereal the bullets must first pass through his body, and at the side of Antonio was his handsome son, Michael. Farther back were the Cornejos, the Hinojosos, the Cepedas, and so on through a list of names which the Kid knew he must memorize before the next day dawned.

Halfway up the hill a halt was made to settle the details of the plan of attack.

"They are all vipers," said Juan Cepeda, his short, iron-gray beard quivering with eagerness of the battle. "Take care, señor, that the life is trod out of every one in the Casa Vereal. Otherwise, they may sting you in the heel!"

"It is true," commented Lope Cornejo, his teeth glinting in a smile of savage malice. "So long as law can be bought and sold, Cabrillo will be formidable with the plunder which he has drained from your estate. Leave no Cabrillo to plead before a judge. Throw a circle around La Casa Vereal like a noose around a rascal's neck. Then we'll draw close in and strangle the life out of them!"

The Kid looked to Halsey, and that worthy nodded eagerly; but still John Jones was not satisfied. Battle, to be sure, he loved with a passionate devotion, but not a massacre such as this promised to be. He allowed such directions to be given, however, as would surround the house, and a broad girdle of yelling enthusiasts was stationed in a solid wall around the great house.

While this maneuver was being carried on, the house remained in silence, saving that a few random shots were discharged on either side, but when the trap was fully set, the Kid ordered all to remain in place until he gave the word to advance. Then, with old Antonio Mendoza, who refused to leave him for an instant, and with young Hernandez Hinjoso also accompanying him, he rode forward to the gate of the Casa Vereal. Twenty men crowded after him, protesting.

"When they see you, señor," cried Cornejos, "one bullet will win their cause."

"You are wrong," said the Kid with more quiet than he felt in his heart. "They know that if they kill me, not a man will escape from the place alive. They are not fools, although they follow Cabrillo."

They could not respond to this argument, and so the Kid came to great barred gate and was challenged from within.

"Send for Señor Cabrillo," he ordered. "Let him know that José Vereal has come to greet his dear cousin."

There was a faint chuckling from the men of San Triste.

"I am Cabrillo," answered a deep and booming voice from behind the gate. "Are you he who claims to be the Vereal?"

"I am Don José," said the Kid simply.

"You are the devil!" roared the other. "My friends, do your duty!"

Here a small door in the gate was opened and half a dozen gendarmes came tumbling forth and headed straight at the Kid, their splendid coats glittering with gold braid and with epaulettes, though their trousers were the cheapest of white cotton and their feet were shoved into the ordinary huaraches.

But they were bold fellows, armed to the teeth with short, heavy sabers and revolvers, and now evidently bent upon a mission which they were determined to perform. They saw themselves upon an important stage, now, with the eyes of the gentry of the city looking upon them, and they were determined to acquit themselves well.

"Keep back!" cried Mendoza, pitching his rifle across the crook of his arm to be in readiness for instant action. "Keep back, policias."

"In the name of the law!" shouted the gendarmes. "Give way."

But they halted, for in the near background they could see scores of steady-handed fighting men ready to rush to the support of their chief.

"Come without fear," said the Kid. "Come to me. You are in no danger."

Mendoza cast a look of wonder at him, while the gendarmes swarmed instantly about him.

"What will you have with me, comrades?" said the Kid.

"You are mad, señor!" exclaimed one of his supporters from the rear.

"I have no fear," said the Kid with some air of solemnity. "The law is my best ally—not my enemy!"

Such assurance took some of the edge of eagerness from the gendarmes, and when he repeated his first question and asked them for what purpose they had come out to him, one of them simply muttered that it was alleged to them that he was not the true Vereal, but an impostor!

"You must be my judges," said the Kid with the utmost good humor. "What? You are not new men! You have seen the Vereals. Look on me, my friends, and tell me whether or no you judge me to be an impostor!"

They stared blankly at him. The voice of Cabrillo roared from his covert: "Your duty, fools!"

"Tell him," said the Kid, "that you serve the law, not one man. I have no doubt that yonder Cabrillo is the man who has testified to you against me; however, your own eye can prove to you that he is a liar!"

Perhaps the gendarmes had little heart for their work from the first; they hesitated for one instant; then they passed over to the side of the Vereal.

"Now, Señor Cabrillo," said the Kid, advancing still nearer to the gate, "I have come to propose terms to you. You have had the use of my properties these dozen years. You have kept yourself and your friends on it. But now that I have returned, I shall not charge anything against you. What you have taken and spent I freely give to you. I make only one demand, and that is for possession of my property on the instant.''

The small door in the gateway opened, and in it stood the formidable figure of Cabrillo, scowling out at his adversary. He was in the most extravagant passion, and though he controlled himself as well as he could, yet his rage made his voice tremble and break as though with terror.

"My friends—my friends!" thundered Cabrillo. "Good gentlemen of San Triste! Have you lost your wits? Are you to believe a lie told you by an impostor?"

"By what right, señor," said Antonio de Mendoza, "by what right do you accuse us of folly? Prove to us that this is not the Vereal. We ask you for that only!"

"Prove to you? I shall prove it!" bellowed Cabrillo.

The blood of the Kid turned cold. He glanced to the side and met the cold eye of Halsey; a little farther away was Marmont, turning pale and setting his teeth. They all recognized the danger. If the Kid were indeed exposed, his life would not be worth a penny for a single second among those determined fellows. They would tear him to bits, showing not the slightest mercy.

Yet John Jones managed to say: "The proof, by all means, Señor Cabrillo!"

Cabrillo drew a great breath as he faced the Kid, and he exhaled again in a single gasp, like a cat spitting defiance, so furious was his temper! His heavy features wrinkled into an expression of the most devilish malice.

First from his lips burst a stream of abuse. Then: "Gallows rat!" shouted Cabrillo. "I shall have you hung for this."

The Kid turned to his companions. "This is an amiable señor, I see," said he. "I have been taught only one way of answering such words, Señor Cabrillo," he continued, facing the big man, "and that is with the language one uses to a horse—so!"

Bringing the black stallion a deft pace nearer, he struck the big man heavily across the face with his quirt. It brought a scream rather of shame and fury than pain from Cabrillo.

From its holster he tore a heavy revolver, and it was well for Manuel Cabrillo that his actions were slow indeed compared with the lightning handiwork of the Kid. That worthy had reversed the quirt with the speed of thought, and, as the gun came from the holster, he brought down the loaded end of the whip across the upper arm of Cabrillo.

It numbed the limb to the fingertips, and the weapon tumbled harmlessly to the ground while twenty sure marksmen, who had twitched up the muzzles of their guns to cover him, relaxed the pressure of their forefingers about the triggers. Cabrillo, amazed and bewildered, rubbed the injured arm, stared down at the Colt upon the ground, and then looked up into the smiling face of the Kid.

That deadly good nature unnerved him more than the black muzzles of the guns which were pointed at him on all sides.

"We have come to understand each other," said the Kid gently. "Now, listen to me: I give you ten minutes to get your papers and your cash together. At the end of that time, my friends of San Triste will close on the house, and I cannot answer for the safety of anyone they find within the walls."

"If we walk out," said Cabrillo gloomily, "what surety do we have that we shall not be murdered?"

"The honor of a gentleman," said the Kid at once, "and the word of a Vereal!"

Saying this he smiled down upon Cabrillo once more. He saw the face of the other turn purple and swell with passion, but even in Cabrillo there was some discretion. He turned on his heel and stalked toward the house, while the Kid turned to confront a storm of protest from his followers.

"If Cabrillo lives," said Hinojoso, "you will be in danger of the rascal every day. As for the other men in the Casa Vereal—"

The Kid raised his hand. He was remembering some of those tales of the Vereal which Joseph Simon had poured into his ears.

"Hush, señor," said he. "There are no doubt very many ruffians and villains among the followers of Cabrillo, but there may also be one or two good men of San Triste with the rest. I could not endanger the life of even one of my children for the sake of ridding us of a hundred enemies.''

15

There is nothing in the world which may be made so soft as the human voice, and of all human voices the softest was that which melted into the sleep of John Jones, alias the Kid. It mingled with his dream; it brought him gently up that steep mountain climb toward consciousness. At last he opened his eyes and was aware that the voice had been intoning the name over and over again, steadily, insistently: ''Señor Vereal— Señor Vereal.''

It was Emile Fleuriot, of course, standing at the foot of the bed, looking down as though he felt it was more delicately proper to be seen than to see in the early morning. The Kid did not speak. He raised himself wearily upon his elbow; a fast, soft pillow was instantly adjusted behind his shoulders and fitted comfortably down into the small of his back.

Then the bony old fingers of Emile Fleuriot held forth the tray on which his cup of chocolate steamed. But not too hot. No, no! There was no fear of that. Neither too hot nor too cool, but just at that proper heat which will warm the body most cheerfully into wakefulness in the dead time of the morning.

The Kid raised the cup slowly from the tray, took a good swallow, and then closed his eyes while he felt that electric heat go through him. His brain, to be sure, was as alert and alive as a wolf's brain when it steps from its lair after sleep, hungry, starved with a three-day fast, ready for the kill; but it would not do to let Emile Fleuriot know this, for this was the third generation which had been served by Emile, and having

been valet to two Vereals in his seventy years of service, it
was to be expected that he knew how men of that blood lived.

For a week, now, the Kid had been studying Emile cautiously,
carefully every day. He had been learning by intuition, well
nigh, exactly what he was expected to do. For his own clear
mind and healthy body, for instance, six hours of sleep every
night was enough, but this would not do. The Vereals were
great sleepers. Therefore the Kid had learned to retire at ten
o'clock of an evening. He slept until twelve.

At the stroke of midnight he wakened, slipped like a cat
from the house, and wandered where he would under the
stars. He was back again in his bed at three; he was wakened
in the morning at seven. This had become a regular program.
But to refuse to retire at ten in the evening would be a shock
to Emile, and he could not risk such shocks.

For already he was beginning to feel that the old valet
suspected something. On this morning, while he closed his
eyes, he glanced cautiously through the lashes and examined
the iron profile of the old fellow with the keenest, tensest
interest. It was a haggard face. Time had wasted the flesh and
loosened the skin into folds. A highlight glistened upon the
cheekbone; darkest shadow lay on the cheek itself; and in
shadow again were the eyes beneath the frowning and bushy
white eyebrows.

They were eyes which always fascinated the Kid, though
they were so far sunken that it was ordinarily hard to examine
them closely. They were extraordinarily thoughtful, and
thoughtful, too, was the great high roomy brow of Emile
Fleuriot, so that even when he stood there holding the
chocolate tray the Kid felt that he had for his valet a
philosopher.

He would never have chosen so imposing an individual,
but he really had no choice; for when it was known that the
Vereal was once again in San Triste, the old servants—all that
were left of them—came hurrying home.

Emile, for instance, had left his pretty little farm in the
valley of the Rhone and his family of grandchildren and his
horses and dogs and the white roads which wound among the

hills he loved. He had left these things sadly, but without a question, to return to the son of his dead master.

Within fourteen days of the moment Emile saw the item in the French newspaper which told of the sudden restoration of the line of Vereal in Mexico, the good old man had landed in Vera Cruz. He had stepped back into his old position with as little question as though he had never left the household. So La Casa Vereal was started again on the oiled wheels of the old service.

The white-haired majordomo, Vasca Corteño, had come back among the first, had wept over his young master, had gone about the house and the grounds of La Casa Vereal, and had cursed the line of Cabrillo to its remotest ancestors because of the changes they had made in the old order of things.

All innovations ceased with the coming of Corteño. He made all as it had been in the good old days. Where former servants had died, he replaced them with new ones. Neither was the will of the new Vereal consulted in these matters, but what Corteño decreed for him and his house was considered good enough.

In short, if he were a king in San Triste, he only presided over a limited monarchy whose ministers held him strictly to account and permitted him only certain liberties in action. He could not order the food which was to be served on his table, because he was given to understand that the Vereal was above such small considerations.

He could not ride his black stallion at his pleasure, because he was informed that the Vereal must not back the same horse more than once a week. Least of all could he dress in what clothes he would, for over this mystery Emile Fleuriot presided with an iron hand.

Meanwhile, Cabrillo had disappeared. The expected contest in the courts did not take place! What the Kid had taken by force he was allowed to keep unmolested. He, Halsey, and Denny, in closest consultation, decided that Cabrillo had been convinced even against his will that the true heir had returned.

In another and greater matter Joseph Simon had taken direction, for when he was informed by a cryptic telegram of

the success of his expedition, he immediately sent back word
that no haste must be used, that the treasure should not even
be searched for until the Kid was firmly established in his
new authority.

It might turn out to be a greater thing than he had at first
assumed. Instead of taking merely the treasure from La Casa
Vereal, it might be that the Kid could obtain permanent
possession of the estate. But let nothing important be done. He,
Joseph Simon, trusting that in the interval of a dozen years
the people of the Mexican city might have forgotten their
hatred of him, would come to San Triste to take active charge
of operations.

"Then," said Marmont, when he received this word, "all
is lost! The fool will not let well enough alone!"

However, they adhered strictly to his orders. It was considered necessary that an intimacy between the Kid and the
three, Marmont, Halsey, and Denny, should grow up gradually.
To the town it was noised abroad that the fondness of the
Vereal for these "gringos" was due to the wholehearted
fashion in which they had supported his cause when he had
reappeared in San Triste.

They began to be seen more and more often at La Casa
Vereal. But still they did not live there, and their business in
the district was vaguely given out as an interest in oil
properties which they were endeavoring to locate.

Such was the condition of affairs as the Kid, on this
morning, peered through his eyelashes at the stern face of his
valet and wondered in his heart of hearts how completely
Emile Fleuriot had accepted him as his true master. For a
week he had striven to come at the truth which must be in the
mind of the valet.

While he finished his chocolate he said to Fleuriot: "Put
down the tray, Emile. There is no need for you to stand and
hold it every morning. The table will do that as well."

Fleuriot became mottled with red. "It is true that I am no
longer young, señor," said he, "but I thank God that I am
not too feeble to hold the tray."

It was always this way with Fleuriot. He acted by a rule
which had been laid down half a century before; to depart

from the rule was to insult him. In the meantime, the Kid heard a faint pattering of feet and the swish of water in the bathroom. For La Casa Vereal scorned modern methods and running water. Every morning for the master's bath the water was heated over the fire and then carried in pails to his tub.

The bathroom was a chamber large enough to have served as a dining hall in a less palatial home. The bath itself was ten feet long and half that width, sunk deep in the floor and composed of huge slabs of the purest white marble. There was a wide, low bench of the same stone covered with thick toweling on which the bather might sit while he dried himself. If the air were chilly of a morning, yonder was actually a fireplace in which the logs were burning with a lavish flame!

The Kid considered these things with a yawn of pleasure, threw off his dressing gown and night clothes, stretched his lithe body from fingertips to toes, and then stepped into the warmed water which lay like a pale blue shadow in the bath.

Later, while he ate his breakfast, the responsibilities of the day began. An alert young secretary, Ferdinand Moya, stood at the side of the table—it would never do to ask him to be seated—and detailed to his master the events of public importance which had been set forth in the last newspaper received from Mexico City.

To this report the Kid listened with much gravity, having decided that a thoughtful air must be his most constant resource while he was carrying on this affair. Breakfast being now finished, the majordomo entered and bowed low to him from the doorway with word of those who waited to see the master of the house and deliver their petitions to him. Vasca Corteño ran through the list.

There was the butcher, Puerillo, who had been ruined by the number of his outstanding bills which he could not collect. A few hundred pesos would save this man and enable him to continue with his shop, which carried on a large trade. The Kid ordered that expenditure. There was Moreño, a small farmer, who had come to the verge of starvation, and who begged for assistance until the next crop; but Basca disapproved of the petition.

"This man is a rascal, señor," he said. "If he is helped

today, he will have to be helped tomorrow. He is the bad penny which comes back often!"

"Has he a family?" asked the Kid.

"A wife and seven children."

"Let the wife and children be cared for; but see that Moreño receives not a penny."

"Señor, it is not wise!"

"It is my will, Vasca."

"It is not wise, señor!"

"Let it be done as I have directed," said the Kid coldly, and Vasca Corteño, growing red with anger, was forced to make that notation.

He went on through the list of the men and women who had come to the Vereal that morning for help; only three were sent away unaided.

When he had ended: "There is one more, señor," said the majordomo.

"And that one?"

"He has come secretly before dawn so that no one in the town could see him. He waits for you now in the little room near the library. It is Cabrillo, señor!"

16

John Jones, alias the Kid, alias José Vereal, received these tidings with a sharp twinge of doubt for what the future might hold in store for him. This return of Cabrillo, secretly, so that no one in San Triste might be aware that he had shamed himself by coming back to one who had so grossly insulted him, might bode almost anything unpleasant.

But, in the meantime, greatly though he yearned to see Cabrillo and learn what mission had brought the latter to

La Casa Vereal, there was another thing which weighed
heavily upon his mind and which he must accomplish this
day.

"Let Señor Cabrillo," he said, "understand that I am
engaged and cannot see him until I return from San Triste. As
you know, Vasca, I am engaged to call upon Señor de
Alvarado this morning."

No doubt Vasca Corteño was a charitable man, but the
pleasant thought of bearing such a rebuff to the former
master of the house made a gleam of malice shine in his
eye. He bowed, therefore, doubly low, and retired from the
room.

The first labors of the morning having passed, the Kid
proceeded to the stables. These stables were large and splendid enough to have formed another mansion almost as preten-
tious as La Casa Vereal, for the Vereal stud had been founded
threescore years ago.

The pick of the Vereal thoroughbreds, since that day, had
campaigned victoriously on many a track, and even Cabrillo
had not dared to break up the expensive stables. San Triste, of
which that stud was one of the greatest prides, would have
risen in instant wrath against the innovator. Even the head of
the stables had not been replaced by Cabrillo, and this was a
little withered Englishman, who had been a jockey in his
youth and then an active trainer on the turf and now was a
peerless stable master.

He had been known as "Red Tom" in his jockey days; now
he was dignified with the title of Señor Thomas Leven. His
flaming hair had rusted and faded to a dull gray. The years
had wasted his body. He was a little cricket of a man with a
sharp, complaining voice that was never amiable until it
touched a horse, and then that voice was a miracle of
gentleness.

"I shall ride the black horse, Pierre," said the master,
when Thomas Leven came before him.

"Señor," said the disagreeable Leven, "you rode the black
horse five days ago."

"It was only a jaunt," insisted the Kid. "Pierre would
laugh at fifty miles a day, for that matter."

"There is too much dust blowing," objected Leven in a tone of almost weary finality. "You would be on a white horse instead of a black one in ten minutes."

"I'll take the chestnut, then," said the master.

"Which chestnut, señor?"

"The big stallion, El Rojo, of course," said the Kid.

"Rojo is off his feed."

"The bay mare, then."

"She is not fit for work. The last time you rode her, señor," continued Thomas Leven gloomily, "her wind was almost broken."

"Give me what you will, then," said the Kid petulantly. "I have exhausted my preferences."

Accordingly, Leven gave orders, and presently a magnificent brown gelding, muscled smoothly and subtly, was led forth saddled and bridled. He stood to taste the wind with his quivering nostrils.

"I'll make out with this," said the Kid, and was instantly in the saddle.

"Steady!" barked Thomas Leven, as though to a groom and not to his own master. "That's not a hobby horse to knock about! He has a spice of devil in him, and—keep away from the spurs. He'll do without them!"

As he said the last of this, his hand fell on the neck of the brown beauty, and the gelding grew instantly quiet.

"Stand back!" said the Kid, tasting the joy of battle in the tremor that ran through him from the quivering loins of the horse. "This horse must come to know me—and my way is with the spurs!"

He used them as he spoke, and the brown sailed like a rocket into the air. Perhaps there was a dash of bronco in the gelding in the dim past. Or perhaps he had seen the mustang perform at a roundup. At any rate, Emperor, for that was his name, twisted and turned and raged like a great cat for half of five minutes.

Half a dozen of the grooms would have rushed to the rescue to catch at the reins of the maddened horse, but Thomas Leven kept them back with his sinister voice: "That's the way of the Vereal," he said. "They learn by breaking their bones. This one is like the others—holla!"

The last exclamation burst from his lips as Emperor dropped out of the air, landed softly, shook himself like a dog coming out of the water, and then galloped meekly away. A low, swinging gate blocked the way. Before it could be opened, the Kid put the brown at it, lifted the gelding over with a touch of the spurs, and disappeared down the road toward San Triste with a twinkling of hoofbeats echoing behind.

"That," cried a groom, "does not sound like broken bones!"

Thomas Leven was still gaping, yet he was one who rarely showed surprise. He forgot the Spanish and lapsed into his own vernacular.

"It ain't possible," said Red Tom. "Emperor is a born bad un, and that lad couldn't have—but he did! The first horseman has come into the Vereal family!"

The astonishment he had left behind him was not at all in the mind of the Kid. He was enjoying the wind in his face, and he raised it to such a purpose that the brown horse was already sweating when it flew into the first street of San Triste. But fast though the gelding raced, there was time for the people in the street to see the gallant figure flash past them, and they smiled at the sight.

The hoofs of the brown gelding, in the meantime, had crashed under the broad archway which led into the court of the Alvarado home. There the rider threw himself out of the saddle and tossed the reins to a mozo. Then, laughing recklessly at the frantic efforts of the servant to control the high-headed horse, he entered the house.

He was led at once to Alvarado and found that gentleman smoking a cigar in his library. For Federico de Alvarado was something of a scholar and the only time his grim face relaxed was when a book was unfolded in his lap.

To Señor Vereal he offered another Havana, but the Kid was already lighting a cigarette, and as he flicked the match into an ash tray he broke at once into the reason of his coming.

"Señor Alvarado," he said, "you have been asked to La Casa Vereal to dine. You have not come. Tell me why!"

Such a question, so bluntly put, was the last thing that Alvarado could have expected, however well he might have guessed the reason for the coming of the new Vereal. He was staggered so that his customary poise for an instant left him.

"I only feared that I might not be truly welcome."

"Because you held back on the first night of my coming? Tush, my friend, that was nothing. I respect a man who insists on taking time for thought. In your eyes I might have been—what? An adventurer." He chuckled.

Alvarado made no answer.

"However," the Kid continued, "I have been hunting about for other reasons for your coldness. At last I think that I have found it. Money, says the old saw, is the root of all evil, and here I have found a record of certain moneys loaned to you by Cabrillo from the Vereal estate."

He drew from his pocket a slip of paper; Alvaredo glanced wildly about him. There was nothing to rescue him from this sudden calamity. Somewhere in the house a door opened; a girl's light voice was singing, and Alvarado turned upon his guest at last.

"It is true, señor, that there is a debt," he said.

"You are wrong," said the Kid. "There is no debt. The fire has it!"

He tore the paper across and tossed it upon the hearth where the soft ashes covered all of it.

Alvarado bit his lip. "The existence or the disappearance of a slip of paper, señor," he said huskily, "does not make the debt a peso less or more."

"Wrong! Wrong!" said the Kid hastily. "A Vereal has no memory of such matters except what his papers may tell him. So, Señor Alvarado—that is no more! I am glad. Come, come, my friend. There are not many names in San Triste, and one of them is Alvarado. You are in trouble. Hush! Ferdinand Moya has told me. That young man is the devil; he knows everything that people would hide from him. He has told me that you are still in debt; unhappy! That is no longer true. There is a Vereal in San Triste, and his fortune is the fortune of his companions!''

Don Federico had bitten his lip until it bled. Pride and shame and sorrow and doubt made his color quickly come and go. But he said at length, looking down to the floor: ''Why will you do all of these things for me?''

''If there were another ear to listen to us,'' said the Kid, ''I never could say what I have. But there is no other. I can pocket my pride. I can say to you, frankly: You were my father's nearest and dearest friend, Señor Alvarado, and you shall be mine also!''

He saw the gleam of the perspiration upon the forehead of the proud Mexican. He saw the slim hand of Alvarado trembling where it rested upon the table. At last the eyes of the aristocrat rose and met his own.

''Señor,'' said Alvarado, ''I shall confess. Until this moment I have doubted—everything! But at last I know that it is the truth; the Vereal has indeed come back to San Triste!''

They shook hands with much solemnity.

''If the ghost of my father,'' said the Kid with all the ardor of hypocrisy, ''looks down on us, he rejoices!''

''Young man,'' said Alvarado, his voice shaken with feeling, ''the ghost of your kind father and my dear friend is already before me and lives in the body of his son!''

He stepped from the room with an apology and came back instantly—so quickly that the shrewd John Jones suspected the lady might have been listening to the talk in the adjoining chamber—with the señora upon his arm.

''My dear,'' said Alvarado, ''I have ceased to doubt. The spirit is too like! God knows with what joy I present to you Señor Don José Vereal!''

What the lady said, John Jones hardly heard, for his spirit was swelling within him and a voice was saying over and over at his ear: ''I have them both in the hollow of my hand. Now for the other.''

17

The lady Margarita Alvarado was speaking.

"Perhaps in your homecoming, you may need a woman's hand about your house, señor," she said. "Then you must remember that Margarita Alvarado is at your service."

"Señora," he answered, "you are a thousand times kind. There is a great problem of a new garden which we are about to wall in and plant—"

"Ah, I am only a stupid amateur as a gardener, señor. But my daughter Alicia—"

The heart of John Jones sang in his breast so loudly that it seemed to him that they must hear the music.

"Then I must see her."

"Whenever you will."

A green canary dropped onto the sill of the open window and sat there rocking lightly in the wind.

"On such a happy morning," said the Kid, "what could be better than to talk of flowers? May I talk with the señorita, then?"

He espied a sharp glance of meaning pass from the lady to her spouse. Let them think what they would; they could not have too deep a meaning to please him. Alvarado was excused to return to his book; for he confessed that he did not care for flowers, and it was in the garden, even at that moment, that they must hunt for Alicia. On the way, the señor made a few explanations.

"Alicia is a simple girl," she said. "In these noisy times,

92

few have a taste for such as she. For the convent quiet is still about her, dear girl!''

John Jones did not speak; he could not. He saw only one thing, and that was the defiant beauty who had stood between her father and the danger of the crowd. But, oh, what a change was waiting for him when he came at last into the garden.

She stood in a corner of the garden and the wind swayed the deep-flounced dress about her slender body and tilted the brim of her Leghorn hat. She came to them, smiling through the shadow which fell from that broad brim, with a trowel in one hand and the other gathering up the skirt, lest it should sweep down the head of some brittle-stemmed flower.

This was not the startled queen he had seen from the street when he sat in the saddle on black Pierre. For she seemed like a picture taken out of some lonely field in the country. She was hardly even more than pretty, until she came near, but when she was close before him, the magic went out from her to John Jones and gathered him in, and he never again in all his life could look at her with unenchanted eyes.

''It is Señor Don José Vereal, Alicia,'' said the señora. ''He and your father have been talking,'' she added with a marked emphasis, ''and I have brought him out to you to talk about gardens and flowers. He is making a new garden in La Casa Vereal!''

Now when Alicia came up to them, the sight of the stranger had made her smile go out, but when her mother had finished speaking, the smile came back most wonderfully and a dimple settled in her cheek.

He was lost; and he rejoiced in the immensity of that sudden loss. He loved her. How sweet it was to know at once that he could never cease from loving.

''All the tales are true, then,'' he heard her say, ''and you are the Vereal!''

''The señor has come to talk of flowers, Alicia,'' said her mother with a pronounced sharpness, as though to call her daughter to herself. She favored Alicia with one look burning with pregnant meaning: ''Your fortune is in your hands, child,'' said that look. ''Do your best!''

Then the señora, like a most wise chaperone, found something to surprise her and interest her in the farther end of the
garden where, in a trice, she was out of sight among some
great shrubs of flowering quince now beautiful with pink
blossoms.

"There is a bench in the shadow of the wall," said
Alicia. "Shall we sit there?"

Past a great cool patch of blue delphiniums they went, and
past a glow of little petunias, purple and pink; until at last
they sat on the bench with a milky cloud of honeysuckle
bloom hanging above them. The strong fragrance drenched
the air; even when the wind blew it could not lift all the
weight of that perfume. But to John Jones, forever and ever,
that fragrance was to mean Alicia.

"Tell me first how big the garden is to be?"

"So big—do you see?"

He drew it on the ground with a hasty finger.

"A hundred feet long and more than half as wide," he told
her.

"Oh," said Alicia, "you can put a whole world of flowers
in that!"

"Tell me what must go in that world. I have paper and
pencil here, you see."

"I hardly know." She dropped her chin upon a small
brown fist and dreamed with the eyes of one who creates a
picture in the inward mind.

"Of course hollyhocks along the wall—there'll be a real
wall, of course?"

"Of course."

"Dobe?"

"Oh, no!"

"Bricks, then? Real, red bricks. Nothing makes so good a
background for green things."

"Red bricks it shall be built of. And hollyhocks against
it?"

"There'll be a fountain, too?"

"Of course!"

"I've seen some jade-green rock in the mountains—"

"I shall send to find it, be sure!"

"What a wonderful garden you will have, señor!"

She turned admiring eyes upon him, and John Jones drew a great breath.

"I have never known a man who cared so for flowers!"

A little green canary dropped out of the wind and swung on a tendril of the honeysuckle close beside them, with its wings spread, twittering.

"Hush!" whispered the girl. "See how bold it is!"

"It is the bird that brings me luck," said John Jones, for it darted into his excited brain that this might be the very wanderer which had perched on the windowsill in the house a few minutes before.

She hardly heard him. She had stretched out her hand toward it, slowly, holding her breath. It gave John Jones his chance to drink in all the beauty of Alicia. She was all new to him.

She turned back to him. "But how many other things can be done! There will be great yellow jonquils, of course. And Hyacinths, and asters and violets—but, señor, señor! You have not written down a single word!"

He stared down in confusion at the blank paper.

"It is all written in my mind."

"Can you remember so much?"

"I swear, señorita—"

She raised a cautioning finger and smiled at him behind it.

"What flower, then, did we choose to plant near the walls?"

He bit his lip. "Hyacinth?" he said with faint hope.

She began to laugh, and he could not tell which was the more delightful—to watch her laughter or to listen to it.

"Why have you come here, señor? It was not to listen to my silly chatter about flowers, I am sure of that."

"You are angry?"

"In San Triste, who can be angry with the Vereal?"

"Now you mock me."

"Truly, no!"

Suddenly he believed her. "If I say, then, that I have come only to hear you talk—about flowers—about anything?"

He watched the color flood from her throat to her face and die away.

"Forgive me! I should not have said that."

"Why is it wrong?" she asked him quietly. "I thought it was a very beautiful thing to say. But did you mean it?"

He knew that she was waiting; he would have given a year of life to know the ten right words to say just then; but he could find nothing. He could not have uttered them even if the inspiration had come.

Then Señora Alvarado came with a spray of the flowering quince in her hand and John Jones rose to his feet.

"How far has the garden grown?" she asked them.

"We have built the wall and planted the flower before it," he told her, a little uncertainly. "Have we not?"

Alicia looked up out of a depth of thought. "Oh yes," she murmured. "We have done that. It will be—a strange garden, mother!"

They went down the path toward the house together until Alicia murmured something and hurried on in front with her head bowed a little in the same deep thought. John Jones saw that the lips of the señora were compressed, but whether it was with excitement or disapproval he could not tell.

But then, because he could not contain himself longer, he turned to her squarely.

"Señora," he said, "I am a stranger to your house before today. I hope that from now on I may come to see you often?"

"We are honored," said she, flushing a little.

He met the question in her eyes, growing a trifle red in turn.

"But I must speak of a certain matter to Señor Alvarado," said he, and went, accordingly, straight to that gentleman, whom he found behind a book, still in the library. Don Federico marked his place with a slim fingertip as he looked up.

"Señor Alvarado," said John Jones, "when I awoke this morning I was what the world calls a rich man; this moment I am a beggar and I have come to tell you that all I have is nothing unless I can have your daughter as my wife!"

Don Federico grew very pale. He closed his book. He

folded his hands upon it. He looked up to John Jones with a sort of sad wistfulness.

"It would be my highest hope," he said. "But it is impossible!"

"In the name of heaven—and why?"

"She is betrothed."

"If she is not married, I shall still hope."

"I have pledged my word. No priest could bind her more surely."

A groan broke from the lips of John Jones.

"To whom, then?"

"To Manuel Cabrillo!"

18

It was said of the new Vereal that he rode like a thunderbolt. He and his horse flashed into view in one instant. The next, the long withdrawing roar of the hoofbeats pounded far away and the rider was already unseen. As he had flashed into San Triste on this day, so he flashed out again with the brown gelding running like mad. Up the hill they flew.

In the stable yard the Kid flung down to the ground and tossed the reins to the groom. That groom was no other than Red Tom Leven, but even Tom Leven had not a word to say.

"What a man needs to make him a man," said Tom Leven thoughtfully, as he watched the Kid stride away toward La Casa Vereal, "is a little sprinkling and salt of the devil in him!"

He nodded as though he certainly believed that the new master possessed this proper seasoning. With the same black face the Kid entered the house and passed Vasca Corteño in the great hall.

"Is Cabrillo still in the same room?" asked the Kid, without lifting his eyes from the floor.

"He has not moved," said Corteño, and studied the face of the master with a covert anxiety.

The Kid went on. He opened the door of the little private chamber which opened off the big library—a chamber constructed by Don Diego in his old age when he found that books were meaning more and people less to him than before. He had set off a corner of the library, therefore, with a thick, soundproof partition. It made a room not more than four paces by three, though the ceiling was of the height of the great library itself and therefore gave the apartment a towerlike interior which pinched the floor space together.

Manuel Cabrillo had fallen into a state of semi-drowsiness, wakened only now and again by a sudden spur of desire for a drink of tequila, which was his favorite beverage.

He had so far sunk in this sleepiness that the soft-footed coming of the Kid hardly aroused him. It was rather like a vision which we see in a dream, the mind dreading it though the body remains inert. But when the Kid closed the door behind him, though it made only the slightest click, yet that small noise of metal on metal was enough to make Cabrillo leap to his feet with a snort of alarm.

The Kid crossed the room to him and shook him by the hand with a lingering grip. Manuel Cabrillo had a horrible feeling that by that handgrip his power had been discovered and found a small, contemptible thing. He could see the Kid smiling down upon him as a giant might smile down on a dwarf, and yet his own bulk was enough to furnish forth almost two of such youths as this. This reflection upon his advantage in physical size comforted Cabrillo a little; but still he could not face the cruel and steady smile of the Kid. It searched coldly into every corner of his brutal soul and told him that he was condemned to destruction.

"Señor," said Cabrillo, "I have come to talk to you about a small agreement which we could make."

"Good!" said the Kid.

He sat down upon the edge of the square table in the center of the room, a table which many an hour of friction against the soft bindings of morocco and levant and glistening, ivory-stained vellum, had polished richly. There sat the Kid, one leg swinging while he viewed Cabrillo with bright eyes of malice.

Let it be said for Cabrillo that he was a man of steady nerves who, before this day, would have found it impossible to even imagine himself shrinking from another man. He had fought before, and more than once, but now he began to revise his judgment of himself, though that is the last thing which any man will do.

To be sure, he had immense and crushing force in his burly hands, but as he considered his companion, he began to have an uneasy sense that it would be most difficult to fasten a grip upon that slender body. Just as the most ponderous mastiff, which will assail any domestic dog without a moment's hesitation, looks with loathing and doubt upon an agile, light-bodied wolf, so Cabrillo looked upon the Kid and doubted himself.

Those long, delicately made hands of the younger man, he told himself, could whip out a gun in the twinkling of an eye; and those keen, steady eyes told Cabrillo that this man would not miss his mark. One bullet would be enough.

"Now," said the Kid, "the agreement?"

"You are a bold man, señor," said Cabrillo. "I am one who admires courage. Since I have lost La Casa Vereal," he went on frankly, "I have been considering how I could regain it, of course."

"Of course," admitted the Kid.

"Because," went on Cabrillo, "the possession of the estate means to me much more than mere money—much, much more!"

The face of Alicia came gently before him like a dream, and he sighed; but here a slight movement of the other made him look up, and he saw in the face of the Kid such a blaze of hatred and contempt and disgust that he shuddered.

"I have it in my power," said Cabrillo, "to take the place away from you."

"Ah?" murmured the Kid.

"But taking it away from you in that fashion, I should be taking it away from myself, also!"

The Kid was silent. Something of his fury was abated, and in its place came a cool, steady watchfulness. Whatever was in the wind, he would be prepared to play his hand to the best advantage.

"In short, señor," said Cabrillo, "I have it in my power to produce the true Don José at any moment!"

It was a thunderbolt, indeed, for the Kid; but he stood the shock without betraying an instant's uneasiness in his eye.

"That's a pleasant story," said the Kid, and waited.

"Of course," said Cabrillo very carefully, as though he were most anxious not to raise the fury of this dangerous enemy, "of course this needs to be explained. Good! To *you*, señor, it will not be hard to tell the whole story truthfully. For you are one who, like me, believes in attaining one's end; the means hardly matter."

He winked broadly at the Kid. The latter said not a word; nothing about him stirred; the cigarette fumed in his hand and the ash grew long and broke off; even his glance had not altered from the face of Cabrillo.

"Very well," said Cabrillo. "We go back, then, to that day a dozen years ago when the revolution struck San Triste, killed the Vereal, stormed his house, and afterward it was found that young José, together with his French tutor, or governor, Louis Gaspard, had disappeared. It was thought at first that their bodies had been consumed when certain out-buildings were burned by the revolutionists.

"That news was brought to me, and I began to prepare to start for San Triste and take possession of the estate as the next heir to the property. I had already received congratulations. That night I was so full of thoughts that I could not remain quietly in the house and wait for the morning. I had a horse saddled and rode out by myself.

"It was a fortunate ride for me. I had passed two miles from the house up the northern road when I saw two horsemen coming slowly toward me with weary horses. I could tell that by the way their heads hung. When they came nearer, I saw that one was a boy and that one was a man. When they came

still closer, I recognized Louis Gaspard, and though I had
never seen young José, I could guess that the boy was he.

"Gaspard was frantic with joy when he saw me. Their
troubles were at an end, he said, and God had saved them
after their wild ride. Little José hardly heard what his tutor
was saying. He had doubled up in his saddle and was half
asleep from exhaustion. They had not quit the saddle except
for a moment now and again, during thirty-six hours. They
had fled like wild men across the countryside, fearing that the
revolution was everywhere around them and that they must be
proscribed, because of that murderous attack against La Casa
Vereal. For the family, they knew, was too rich to be safe
during a time of revolution.

"For my part, while I listened to Gaspard, I was thinking a
great many unpleasant thoughts. For there were an old man
and a young boy, both helpless. If they were removed, I was
still to be congratulated for having come into the possession
of La Casa Vereal. Such were the thoughts that went through
my mind, of course."

"Of course," said the Kid without emotion. "To put a pair
of bullets into the two of 'em and have no more to worry
about.'

"You are precise, señor. That was of course my idea. But
even a strong man will have, on occasion, his weak moments.
I, on that evening, thinking the matter back and forth, had a
qualm—partly of conscience and partly of fear of the results.
A bold and careless man like yourself, señor, would not have
been so troubled?"

"Perhaps not," said the Kid, and lighted another cigarette
from the butt of his first.

"The man was very old, ' went on Cabrillo, explaining his
weakness with some care, as though it were a thing of which
he might well be ashamed in the view of such a listener as the
present. "The boy was very young. Besides, I had known
Gaspard for some years, and I had always found him courte-
ous and gentle. Had he been something above a tutor in a
private family, one might have felt him to be a·gentleman!"

The Kid nodded.

"In short, I was not able to draw my gun upon them,

though I confess that my fingers itched to wrap themselves around the butt. However, before long I thought of another alternative. I drew Louis Gaspard aside. I said to him: 'Louis Gaspard, you are an old man.'

" 'I am,' said he in his soft voice, looking up at me from under his white bush of eyebrows.

" 'But still,' said I, 'you have many years before you. You are healthy. Your eye is as clear as the eye of a young man. You have good habits. You do not drink too much; you smoke only a little.'

" 'One cigar each day, only,' said Gaspard. 'Why do you say these things, Señor Cabrillo?'

" 'Because I have your welfare at heart,' said I. 'I should say, now, that you are a man who finds great pleasure in your work.'

" 'Who would not?' said he. 'I take the mind of a little child, unformed and without thoughts—only with feelings. Here is something which may be made to think thoughts, and thoughts are a power which turns the world.

" 'A man ten thousand miles away may think a thought which will change your life and mine when he has expressed it. My duty is to train the young mind of the boy so that it may grow up into a strong mind as a man. You will see that there is nothing so important in the world as this.'

" 'It must be a great satisfaction,' said I.

"He shook his head, at that, and sighed a great sigh.

" 'There are too many troubles which come between me and my work,' said he. 'I am employed by rich men. The sons of rich men are my pupils. Why should they work? Why should they study? They inherit enough wealth to give them fine food, fine clothes, excellent servants and, above all, the respect of their fellow men. That is an ungrateful soil for me to work, and where I plant seeds of wheat I too often see only rank weeds grow up!'

"I saw that he had grown enthusiastic. Think of it, señor! After passing through the danger of death; after having saved from the massacre this boy; after having ridden for a day and a half with hardly a pause, this Frenchman could forget everything and talk only about his work! I wondered at him then as you will wonder now!

"Then I saw that, through his talk, he had placed in my hands the very thing for which I wished. It was a leverage to loosen him from his honesty—a small leverage, but perhaps enough.

"I said to him: 'Gaspard, suppose that this boy who is with you were to lose all his money; what could be done with him then, if you could afford to educate him?'

"Gaspard comes from Normandy; and a Norman thinks of money as a woman thinks of love.

"'If I could afford to educate him for nothing, have him utterly in my hands, I could make of him a great man, señor. But he is cursed—I whisper it to you—because since the death of his poor father, he is the Vereal!

"I thought upon this for a moment. You will have seen, by this, that Gaspard was an odd man; perhaps his brain was a little touched. Between you and me, I think that is too often true of people who spend a great deal of their time over books. Consider: Would not a man go mad if he were always made to listen and could never talk back? That was the way with poor Gaspard. However, it was a useful madness to me.

"Then I said to him: 'Louis Gaspard, there is a way in this thing by which you may be served, because you are an honest man and wish nothing but good to your pupil; I also may be served who am not quite so honest and who am more ready to serve myself. Suppose that you were to take your boy, young José, and go with him into some other country—some country to the south, perhaps.

"'There you could sit down with him and lead a happy life. You would receive from me an ample income. How much, Louis Gaspard, do you make now? Three thousand? We will quadruple that. You will receive twelve thousand dollars a year from me, and out of that money you will have to support only yourself and young Don José!'

"He could only stare at me for the time. He turned red with thinking me a rascal; but he turned white again when he thought of the twelve thousand. Besides, he saw my hand upon the butt of my revolver, and I suppose that he knew without much thought that I would probably put them both out of my way with the gun if he did not accept my proposition. But after he had looked at me for a long time, he said, like a true Norman: 'How can I be sure that the money will be sent to me?'

" 'My word of honor,' said I.

"Here the rascal had the presumption to smile in my face.

" 'Very well,' said I. 'I shall give you a signed contract.'

" 'Very well,' said Louis Gaspard. 'After all, it is for the good of little José.'

" 'You will both change your names,' said I.

"He nodded.

" 'You will travel to a place which I shall name. There you will stay. You will make little José feel that it is now dangerous for him to be known as a Vereal because of the revolution. He is barely ten now, and he is not a very bright boy; in a few years this will all be like a dream to him unless something happens to make him remember.

" 'You will guarantee that?' said I.

"He said that he would, and that for twelve thousand a year, he would guarantee to do even more. Young Don José should grow up with a new name and the past should be rubbed out of his mind.

" 'But alas,' said Gaspard, 'you are making a villain of me!'

" 'I am showing you your way to good fortune; that is all,' said I.

"That was how I persuaded Louis Gaspard. To show you how mad he was: He was willing to risk his life, as he had actually done, to save young José from the revolutionists; but yet he would sell all of his honesty for the simple matter of twelve thousand a year, while he gave me millions! Yes, señor, when I think back to it, I marvel at that man! For the interest upon a scant two hundred thousand, he gave me the whole huge estate.

"Upon my soul, I think he hardly thought of the thing. You will see how it was. Twelve thousand was a million to him. It was his price. When I hit that price, he dissolved. If I had said more, it would have frightened him. If I had said less, he

could have afforded to grow indignant and would have been
apt to die for his honest principles. But as it was, I named the
exactly correct sum. He was fascinated by it. After that, he
could not resist me!''

19

Reconsidering the perfect skill with which he had tempted
and bought poor Louis Gaspard, Cabrillo sighed with pleasure and began to rub his huge hands together.

''However,'' said the Kid quietly, ''twelve thousand a year
is a good deal to pay.''

''Of course,'' agreed Cabrillo hastily. ''But Gaspard was
so old; who could have thought that he would live these
dozen years? When he died I would have let young José take
care of himself and make his own way in the world, of
course!''

''Of course,'' agreed the Kid in his matter-of-fact voice.

''However, you can judge of yourself by this letter.''

He passed an envelope to the Kid and the latter read the
enclosure. It was written in a fine hand, the lines only a little
tremulous, but the letters still so carefully drawn that they
might have served as copy to a youth studying penmanship.
The letter acknowledged the last remittance and thanked
Cabrillo for his usual promptness. It went on to state that
Señor Don Felipe Carvajal continued to improve in his studies
and in his exercises and had become a perfect example of all
that a young gentleman should be.

For his own part, Louis Gaspard found himself in constantly
improving health and had nothing to wish for. He had
accomplished, he felt, the perfect labor for which all of his
life had been given. He had created by his teachings, a

gentleman and a scholar so exquisitely finished that he
desired now to live only long enough to see the world
acknowledge and give a great place to his masterpiece.

For, though Felipe steps forth into a degenerate world, a
hard and a cruel and a suspicious world, he will make his
way. There is still a recognition of merit and of genius. For
the great estate which I have caused him to lose, I have not
the slightest regret. If it had not been for that loss, he
would not now be furnished with all the wealth of great
treasures with which his mind is furnished.

As for his education, Señor Cabrillo, he is at ease in the
books and the tongues of three modern languages besides
his own; he is grounded in philosophy, in mathematics, in
music, and in science.

You will expect that his body has been neglected, but I
hasten to assure you that this is not the case. I have seen to
it that he should be given a healthy body to reënforce the
activities of his brain. He has been prepared for boxing and
wrestling under professional instructors. He rides with the
wildest courage and the strangest skill; he is part of the
animal on whose back he sits. He has been trained in the
use of firearms, and with his sure eye and his steady
nerves, his skill has become an amazing thing.

In a word Señor Cabrillo, when you see the young man
who knows himself as Felipe Carvajal, you will see my
conception of the perfect man created in actual flesh and
blood!

Over this portion of the letter the Kid mused for a time, but
at length he lifted his large, somber eyes and dwelt on the
face of Cabrillo.

"It is true, señor," he said quietly, and Cabrillo drew a
great breath of relief, knowing that his story was accepted *in
toto* through the means of that single letter. He had expected
to meet a far more skeptical judge.

"This, then," said Cabrillo, "is what I have done. The
moment I knew that I was overturned by your clever imposi-

tion upon the people of San Triste, I sent for Gaspard and young José—or Felipe, as he is now called!''

He paused and waited for the shock to unsettle the Kid, but the latter did not stir. He was as steady as a soldier sighting a rifle.

''When he comes,'' said the Kid, ''he takes the property from both of us and leaves us with nothing.''

''You are wrong, señor. There will be his gratitude to me for having restored him to his place! I can claim a great deal for that gratitude.''

''There will be his gratitude, also,'' said the Kid, ''for having kept him from his rights for a dozen years. I think you can claim a great deal for that, also!''

Cabrillo scowled. He made an impatient gesture. ''I have thought of that, too,'' he said. ''In the meantime, I am very thirsty. Let me have a glass of tequila, my friend!''

The tequila was brought, and Cabrillo dashed it off with one of his characteristic gulps.

''In the meantime,'' said the Kid, who had joined his guest with a taste of wine only, ''in the meantime, the real Vereal is coming rapidly toward San Triste?''

Cabrillo squirmed in his chair. ''He is coming,'' he said. ''However, there is still something which may be done!''

The Kid smiled. ''I was sure,'' he said, ''that you would not hang both of us with one rope!''

Cabrillo flushed, and then suddenly grinned. ''In a word,'' he said, ''this is what I have done. I have appointed a certain place at which I am to meet Gaspard and José Vereal. If I am not there, they will find a letter awaiting them from me. In that letter Gaspard will be told to reveal to the Vereal his true name and rights. Gaspard will also be told that the reason he receives the letter is because I am not there in person; and that the reason I am not there in person is that I have been destroyed because of intending to tell the truth to poor young José!''

As he spoke the last words, Cabrillo leaned a little forward in his chair. But the Kid did not care to deal in innuendoes for the moment. He smiled grimly upon his guest.

''In that case, I must not kill you, Cabrillo.''

"I am glad that you see," Cabrillo said. "Consider, then, that Gaspard and José are rapidly approaching a certain place which is well known to me. But in the meantime let us reach an agreement. You see that although you hold San Triste, I hold a card which will take your trick. Very good, señor. But it is foolish for us both to give up great wealth. Agree, therefore to take a certain sum of money. Agree to take a mortgage, if you wish, against the estate. Place the figure high.

"I do not care about a few tens of thousands one way or another. This adventure shall enrich you. But agree, having taken an ample sum in cash and in the mortgage, to withdraw from San Triste and surrender La Casa Vereal and the estate back to me. You have the money for which you came, and I have enough left to content me."

"And then José?"

"I meet him and Gaspard. I tell Gaspard that I have sent for him simply because I have decided that they should change their residence to another country—to France or to Spain. That is all! They depart. You take the cash agreed upon; I retain the estate; and all is well!"

"Excellent!" murmured the Kid. "But suppose that I offer you the cash, Cabrillo, while I keep the estate. Would that suit you?"

"Never!" bellowed Cabrillo, and his face grew purple.

The Kid, watching carefully, understood. To hold the position if not the title of the Vereal was what Cabrillo, at any price, desired. It gave him personal greatness in the eyes of the town, even if the town of San Triste continued to hate him. It gave him, above all, the delicate lady, Alicia de Alvarado, to be his wife! The Kid grew as cold as steel.

"It cannot be, Cabrillo," he said. "Be wise. Take the money; take the same mortgages which you suggest to me. But I have grown fond of this old house. It means more than money to me. I am determined to have it—or nothing!"

"Wait!" said Cabrillo. "You are not mad, señor?"

The Kid shrugged his shoulders. He could see Cabrillo trembling with passion, but still restraining himself.

"I repeat it, Cabrillo."

"Fool!" yelled Cabrillo. "You will throw all away, and keep nothing!"

"Would you do the same thing?" asked the Kid.

"Bah! I have enough property in my own name. This is luxury, not necessity to me. But you—what have you besides your hopes in this adventure?"

"A horse," said the Kid, as coldly as before, "and a gun!"

Cabrillo turned from red to yellow. "Is that all?" he asked. "You have made up your mind?"

"And you?"

"I swear to you, señor, that if I cannot have the house for myself, then the real Vereal shall have it!"

"Adios, amigo!"

An indescribable sound burst from the throat of Cabrillo, a throat-glutting exclamation which had no meaning saving animal rage and hatred. Then he hurled his bulk through the doorway. His heavy shambling steps sounded through the hall, and he was gone onto the hard flagging in the patio.

The Kid did not follow. He remained for a moment seated upon the side of the table until through the open window there blew a breath of fragrance from the garden outside, and stronger than all else, the unmistakable sweetness of honeysuckle. At once it seemed to him that he was breathing of the very presence of Alicia, as though all her beauty stood like a ghost beside him.

To lose all the rest was nothing, but to lose Alicia was terrible indeed! He had felt, a short hour before, that her betrothal to Cabrillo was a great obstacle. But now that seemed nothing at all, in the light of the new calamity which was about to fall upon him. A bullet could have ended the other problem; a bullet could not save him from this!

He went slowly out into the library, and there stood the tall form and the pale, stern face of Emile Fleuriot. What had brought and kept the valet there? A chill struck through the Kid, and it was only partly dissipated when Fleuriot announced that Señor Marmont had called on the Vereal.

In another moment Pierre Gaston Marmont entered the room and stood there leaning on his cane.

"Jones!" breathed Marmont. "Have you had a chance to talk to the señoritas?"

Again the wind breathed through the room the rich perfume of the honeysuckle, and the Kid felt his face grow white. So he yawned and covered his mouth.

"Women don't take up my time," he announced.

"Nor mine," answered Marmont quickly. "You can tuck a woman into five minutes of foolishness every day. Still—they have a place!"

He laughed at John Jones.

"You have run out of money again?" said the Kid dryly.

"I need only a trifle," said Marmont airily. "Five hundred pesos will equip me. From my share in the loot, you shall have six hundred to replace the money. Will you believe me, dear friend Jones?"

The Kid drew out a wallet and counted out some bills. "Here is three hundred," he said.

"Only three?" asked Marmont, frowning. "Consider, Monsieur Jones, am I not to be trusted?"

"Tomorrow," said the Kid, smiling faintly, "you may have the two hundred."

Marmont, having reddened a little, then broke into a laugh of the greatest good nature.

"You are right," he conceded.

"Unless," said the Kid, "I haven't the money to give you. We may all be riding for the border before tomorrow night."

"*Nom de Dieu!* What is it?"

"Get Denny and Halsey. Then we'll talk it over."

"Halsey is away until the morning."

"We must wait for him."

"Monsieur Jones!" cried Marmont with a gesture of the wildest dismay.

"Not a word! But one thing more. Go into the little room, there, and close the door which closes on the library, here. Then stand near the table and speak—quite loudly."

Marmont darted a penetrating glance and then obeyed without a word. Presently he reopened the door from the little private library.

"I couldn't hear you," said the Kid. "But go back and speak again."

The door closed and this time the Kid stepped close to it. His ear was not beside the crack nor at the keyhole, yet he distinctly could hear Marmont say in the adjoining chamber. "It is very hot."

The Kid instantly realized the force of those words, for a hot perspiration poured out on his brow. He wiped that moisture away, gloomily, thoughtfully. It all depended on where the valet had stood. If he had been in the center of the room, he could have heard nothing; if he had been close to the door, he might have heard more than enough!

20

All of San Triste walked in the Plaza Municipal in the evening, and the Kid remembered this when, as he paced restlessly in the garden after the coming of the dark, the wind carried to him, faint and far from the town, the thin, sharp whistle of the piccolo, like that same weird high tenor note which is in the Mexican's voice. It was only a strain; he could not hear it again; but in five minutes he was in the saddle, sweeping down toward San Triste. He dismounted at the edge of the Plaza Municipal and joined the promenaders.

There were two main streams of them, walking by the light of the oil lamps, and looking pygmy small under the great alamos. On the inside walk of the boulevard by far the largest and thickest stream was composed of the lower classes; on the outer walk moved all that was highest of the blood of San Triste.

Even in their promenade, however, they moved according to rules. The inner current was composed of the ladies,

the girls and their duennas taking the air under the shelter of
the black lace mantillas; the outer current consisted of the
cavaliers, old and young, but never a man and a woman
walking together. No, if lovers met, it was only for a single
glance, now and again, as the two currents passed, for the
ladies walked ever to the right and the men ever to the left.

For two hundred years men and women and boys and girls
had strolled thus, after the heat of the day, in the Plaza
Municipal, wearing deep, smooth hollows in the limestone
blocks which paved the boulevard; and the Kid felt himself to
be a part of those two centuries of beautiful leisure.

He had walked once before in the Plaza Municipal, and
there he had found that it was the one spot in San Triste
where he would not be followed and embarrassed by the very
weight of affection and respect of the people, for during that
evening promenade, rank and importance disappeared while
there remained only the individual.

Even the individual was not he of tomorrow or of yesterday,
for each man was valued according to the gaiety of his
conduct and his air for that night alone. The Kid, feeling for
the time thoughtful and composed, had only to wrap himself
in his cloak and fix his gaze straight before him in order to be
almost utterly ignored. Men were not willing to meet those
somber eyes, and if they showed their respect for the Vereal,
it was only by keeping a slight distance from him on every
side.

The voices were not loud. The music from the center of the
Plaza, hidden behind the growth of shrubs and trees, dominated.
There was always the shrill note of the piccolo, dear to all
Mexicans; sometimes beneath it one distinguished most clearly the deep and snoring tone of the bass viol; sometimes it
was the beat of the guitar; sometimes it was the sweet, high
singing of the violin, or all these voices blended.

Under cover of that music, men and women whispered and
told their jests and their gossip, and as the double streams
flowed past, the ladies looked fixedly before them; the men
looked fixedly at the ladies. There could have been nothing
more carefully in the bounds of propriety, and yet there was a
sort of childish mischief in the air.

John Jones, for all his abstraction, was scanning from the corner of his eye every face among that drift of ladies. He saw many a graceful form and many a lovely face, but still he searched for something which was missing until, suddenly, he found it. The dull and murky light of an oil lamp fell upon her face and he saw, with a great leap of the heart, that she, too, was covertly watching the faces of the men as they sauntered past her—watching them with a sort of fear. She seemed to John Jones like a single rose in a garden overgrown with weeds.

Had she seen him? "She will look!" he said with a sort of trembling boldness to his heart, and indeed as he passed, her head turned, for an instant their eyes shocked, their steps faltered, and then they went on.

John Jones, dizzy with happiness, drew out from the crowd of the promenaders, and at the very same instant he saw Señora de Alvarado support Alicia out of the tangle of strollers. Two mozos hurried up. He saw the señora giving swift directions; one of the servants raced away. But the heart of John Jones rose cruelly high. He knew well what that sickness was. For he himself was giddy and weak and his pulse fluttered and leaped. He was beside them instantly, his hat sweeping into his hand.

"Alicia has turned sick," said the señora hastily. "I have sent for the carriage, but if you will help us to that bench, Señor Vereal—"

He drew the arm of Alicia within his own and felt the tremor of her body close to his.

"I am quite well," she was whispering. "I need no help."

Yet half of her weight was on his arm as he led her to a place on one of those stone seats which bordered the most outward walk, well removed from the promenaders. The mother leaned over the girl, solicitous and worried.

"I have never seen her like this!" she assured John Jones. "I have never seen her so taken, Señor Vereal. What can it be?"

"It is a warm night," said John Jones. "There was no stir of air for a moment. Perhaps that is it!"

"Perhaps. Alicia, my dear, are you better?"

"Oh, much better!"

"I believe you are. Your color is returning. How fortunate that we met you, Señor Vereal!"

Someone was approaching in haste; the señora turned to announce to the newcomer that Alicia was only slightly indisposed.

"There is no need to keep you here, señor," said a faint whisper beside John Jones. "I am very well, now, Señor Vereal!"

"I shall stay, señorita."

He said it fervently, and as a deep reward he heard her draw a hasty breath.

Then: "I shall explain at another time. But now I beg you to forgive me if I ask you to withdraw, señor."

"Ah, señorita, I am strangely sick and weak. I beg you to allow me to remain a moment to recover."

She looked up at him with a wildness of fear and of doubt. Far away, it seemed, he could hear the mother laughing with the stranger who stood before them; and John Jones could not keep back the words, for they swelled in his heart until it ached and then passed suddenly from his lips against all his volition.

"Alicia—" he whispered, "God has disposed of me."

Far off the piccolo shrilled into a sudden riot that made them both tremble.

"No, señor! No, no—José!"

The name, which was not his, coming from her lips, seemed to John Jones like a baptism. It gave him a right to the title. He felt in a sudden whirl of emotion that her belief made him truly the Vereal.

The carriage swerved up to them and the mozo leaped down.

"God has disposed of me," whispered John Jones again. "From the first glance, I was yours, Alicia. Tell me if I may hope?"

She had no time to answer. Her mother upon one side and the mozo on the other raised her and assisted her into the victoria, while John Jones stood by with a white face, and the brim of the sombrero crushed in his hand. The driver gathered the reins, the victoria began to roll, but as it moved away she turned her head toward John Jones with a look of such happiness and of such trust that he knew it was double magic which had worked upon them both and the treasure was his if he could but claim it.

But trouble had not ended for Alicia on this strange evening, for in another moment the crisp voice of her mother spoke, lowered so that the two servants on the driver's seat might not hear. "My dear, what has become of your illness? You are smiling like a happy child with a new toy!"

"It is the wind which has just sprung up, mother," said Alicia.

"Listen to me!" said the señora. "It is the breath of the words of Señor Vereal."

Alicia sank back into the seat with a murmur of dismay.

"Tell me, child, what he said?"

"He said—nothing. He merely hoped for my recovery."

"His hope was soon fulfilled," said the mother dryly. "Come, Alicia, be open with me!"

"Mother, mother," whispered the girl, "I did not dream that there could be so much happiness in the world!"

The señora stiffened in her place and her eyes blazed. "By heaven," she murmured, "he has made a declaration!"

"He loves me, mother."

"After seeing you twice? This is a pretty thing, indeed; and after your father has betrothed you to Manuel Cabrillo!"

Alicia made a vague gesture.

"Do you not care?"

"I shall not be married to Cabrillo. Now that José has spoken, I belong to him."

"It is well that your father cannot hear you. He would go mad!"

"Do you wish it, also? Will you have me married to Cabrillo?"

"That—pig?" exclaimed the mother. She shuddered. "God forbid! But do you know your own mind, silly girl? What can make you sure that he is not playing with you—this fiery, wild-riding Vereal of whom no one knows anything?"

"I only know this," said Alicia quietly, "that if he will not have me, I shall never wed. If he will not marry me, I shall be happier to die!''

After this, Madame Alvarado said not a word until she was leading her daughter into the house, but as they reached the door she whispered: "Have courage, Alicia, and allow me to manage this thing. You will not die, my dear. Let me handle your father. Even a man's pride is manageable!''

21

Over the northern hills came a tall gray horse with a short-legged rider in the saddle, an uneasy rider who had twisted and turned to find an easier seat and had not succeeded until at last he gave up in despair and remained in one place.

He had ridden most of the night, and now it was nearly mid-morning, yet the gray horse, tougher than steel and with an unfailing heart of high courage, continued to press against the bit, while the rider held it wearily back to a walk. Even the roll and slight jar of a walk was torture to that inexpert equestrian; a trot he dared not venture. His vitals ached with the sway of the body of the gray; even the back of his neck was sore.

He came around the shoulder of a hill and drew rein. There was San Triste spread beneath him, shining the purest white in the early brillancy of the morning sun. The rider rubbed his fat hands together and then went on until he saw a dust spot before him down the winding road. At this he stopped the gray again, but finally went on, rather pale of face, but determined.

The dust spot grew, turned whiter, larger, and finally the shape of a man was distinguishable in it, urging a horse up the slope. They came closer. The mustang was blackened and dripping with sweat, but still the rider put it cruelly to the work of mastering the up-slope as quickly as possible. He hailed the stranger with a gesture; the man on the gray returned the salutation and was riding by when he felt a sudden, probing glance from him who bestrode the mustang. He allowed the gray horse to break into a gentle jog trot; behind him he knew that the man on the mustang had stopped his horse; then he was aware that the other had turned to follow at a not too discreet distance.

With a whiter face than ever, the traveler went on. The road dipped into the foothills. Then another dust spot appeared before him and he shuddered from head to foot. This time it was a group of three riders. They, too, saluted him with the utmost good cheer when he was at a little distance, but when he came closer, two among them reined suddenly back.

"You are Joseph Simon!" cried one, in a voice almost equally expressive of horror and anger.

He on the gray horse shook his head, endeavored to smile, and jogged on, but though he was unmolested, after a time he turned his head enough to see that the three had encountered the first man who had accosted him, and the heart of Joseph Simon turned to dust and ashes.

"They have not forgotten me!" he gasped out, and suddenly he forgot all the small aches in his body.

There was only a brief conference among the four, and then they began to canter their horses sharply down the trail. Joseph Simon did not await their coming. He leaned forward, screamed in the ear of the gray, and the next instant was almost torn from his seat by the forward lurch of his horse. At the same time, a wild yell rose from the four who followed in his wake.

He glanced back, as he scrambled into the saddle and shoved his feet firmly into the stirrups once more. They were riding like wild Indians behind him, and there was already a gun in each hand. He could see the weapons wink and shimmer in the morning sun, and, desperate at that sight, he urged the gray forward still faster.

His pursuers did not gain. He could see that. For though the gray might be weary from the long journey, blood and length of legs would tell in the first sprint, at least. That sprint saw the gap between the gray and the mustangs greatly lengthened, and though by this time the tall horse began to labor in its stride, on the other hand La Casa Vereal was now not far away, and toward it Joseph Simon streaked across the country. He reached the bridge across the Rio Sabrina. The hoofs of his horse beat up the hollow echoes. He swept on, clattering over the rocks, and the gray leaned to the labor up the long hill.

Behind him the four mustangs crashed across the bridge, each taking the lead from the other, red-eyed with the fury of running and now gaining fast upon their prey. But still they were far away. Even the fierce hearts of those riders saw that they could not win, and therefore a gun spoke, something whizzed above the head of Joseph Simon, and he flattened himself along the neck of his horse, with a groan of terror.

There was another crackling roll of gunfire; wasp voices hummed bitterly around Simon. Then he saw before him the great entrance gate of the Casa Vereal and dashed through it.

In the court he encountered no other person than Vasca Corteño, in the act of delivering a lecture to the downheaded group of gardeners, who had been neglecting their duties in some small particular. But the old man broke off with a muffled cry of anger when he saw the newcomer.

"Simon!" he said. "The evil days have come back upon us. Joseph Simon!"

Simon dropped from the saddle and staggered—almost fell.

"There are brigands—murderers who have chased me— call the Vereal—save me—kind Corteño!"

"Dog!" said Vasca Corteño through his teeth. He added aloud: "They will not dare pursue you into La Casa Vereal. But if you will take an honest man's advice—keep far from San Triste. There are five thousand men near you who would make a target of you, Joseph Simon!"

Simon groaned; even the gardeners he eyed with suspicion, and they glared evilly back at him, for they were among that old force of servants whom he had discharged from the service of the Vereal fifteen years before. Much as Vasca hated him, he knew that Corteño was telling him the best truth for the safety of his skin, but he had come for something which was almost as dear as life.

He demanded to be led to the Vereal at once. Vasca Corteño told him that he would be announced and soon came back into the courtyard to state that the Vereal would presently be at leisure.

"Presently?" burst out Simon, full of wrath. "I have come a long journey to see him!"

"I have no doubt," said Corteño, and could not repress a smile of malice. So a long half hour dragged by before Simon was actually sent for and brought into the library where the Kid awaited him. The door had no sooner closed upon Vasca Corteño than Simon burst out: "What is the meaning, Mr. Jones? Why am I kept like a fool, waiting even outside the house while you—you—smoke another cigarette!"

"Simon," said the Kid in his smooth voice, "in San Triste, I am José Vereal."

Simon straightened. "Very good," he said, smiling, "but these walls are thick, Jones!"

He added: "However, I am here. Heavens knows that I was within an inch of death half a dozen times in the last hour, but I'll forget that. What matters is that you have done everything magnificently. I heard as I traveled. The air was full of it. The true Vereal has returned to San Triste, more generous than all of his ancestors!"

He dropped into a chair chuckling. Then he burst out with irrepressible anxiety. "But that which is under the house!" he asked, pointing down.

"We have not even looked for it. We waited for you to come. It would not do to rummage about the house until there was absolute need."

"Very wise," said Simon. "And the three?"

Instead of answering, the Kid crossed the room and opened the door of that little private chamber which adjoined, and there stepped forth Halsey, Marmont, and Silas Denny, one by one. Prosperity sat visibly upon them, for enough of the Vereal gold had already stuck to their fingers to make itself noticeable in their clothes and in their manner. They greeted Joseph Simon each after his own fashion, Marmont bowing,

Halsey waving an airy hand, and Silas Denny favoring him
with a huge, bonebreaking grip.

"Now that we're all here," said the Kid, "I can tell you
that the game is on its last legs."

The three looked at one another; Joseph Simon, very pale,
got up from his chair and moved his lips without making a
sound.

"Cabrillo has come back to me," said the Kid. "He
wanted to give me a lot of hard cash and mortgages on the
rest of the estate if I'd turn it back to him and disappear out
of the country. He had this trump in his hand: He has the real
Vereal up his sleeve. He can produce him at any time!"

"And you? And you?" murmured Joseph Simon.

"I offered him the same terms if he'd shuffle his real Vereal
out of sight and keep him there."

"Why that?" asked Halsey. "Will you trade a million or
so against a comfortable house—when the house is liable to
be taken from you at any time?"

"I'll make that trade," answered the Kid.

"Did he prove that he had José?" asked Simon.

"He did."

"That he could prove the identity of José to the world?"

"He has Louis Gaspard with José."

There was a groan from Simon.

"He would not take the cash for his share, then?"

"No. He left in a rage."

"How soon can he bring in José? Have we time to get even
the treasure out of Mexico?"

"I don't know."

Joseph Simon walked up and down the room. Now and
then he raised his clasped hands above his head. But finally he
turned violently upon the Kid.

"Mr. Jones, had you a right to make bargains for yourself?
Would you ever have been placed in this house if it had not
been for me?"

The Kid was proof against passion. But he slipped back
into a corner of the room so that he would have all four of the
men directly in front of him and they, subtly enough, felt that
this was a sort of declaration of independence. Henceforward,

no matter what they might do, the Kid was only partly with them. He had established a goal and a policy of his own.

"You sent me down here," said the Kid slowly, "and all that I had with me was a resemblance to the Vereal family. What I gained, I gained by myself. Marmont and Denny and Halsey were no help. I played the part, raised the mob, drove Cabrillo out of Casa Vereal, and won over San Triste.

"Now, Simon, I intend to hold what I have won. I had one chance in two of keeping it before Cabrillo told me about the real José Vereal. After he told me that, I saw that I had only once chance in twenty. But I intend to stay here on the ground and play that one chance out for what it's worth. That's flat!"

"Fool!" burst from the lips of Joseph Simon.

"Perhaps," said the Kid. "But in the meantime, if your money is in this house, get it and cart it out of Mexico. My share in the stuff I turn over to the three others. I'll furnish the pack mules and the muleteers. I'll stay behind to keep some of your friends in San Triste from following."

Here he turned to Simon with a mirthless smile. "Otherwise, if you think that I'm getting what I shouldn't have, you can all stay here and take your chances with me when the real Vereal shows up."

They regarded him as they would have regarded a madman. Joseph Simon counted out the points on the flat of his hand, stabbing the forefinger of his other hand into it savagely.

"You could have made it safe and sure to get this money out of Mexico. You could have had what I've promised you—and that's enough to keep you from starving the rest of your life! Instead of that, you let Cabrillo call in the dog on us and spoil the game for us all! We need time. We can't get seventy mules together, pack them, and move them out of San Triste and over the border in a minute, and José Vereal will be here at any time! Jones, are you mad?"

"Perhaps," was all the Kid would say.

Then Marmont exclaimed: "There is a woman in it. Who can hold the pace when a woman mixes in?"

The Kid turned the talk from himself effectually enough. "In the meantime, we're not sure that the money is in La Casa Vereal!"

"Sacré bleu!" murmured Marmont. "If it is gone, Monsieur Jones—"

His eyes darted a threat at the Kid which that young worthy shrugged away with a perfect indifference. Nevertheless he knew that unless the treasure were found, he would be accused of having moved it away.

22

They went at once to the cellar of the house where Joseph Simon took the lead. He guided them to a corner door which, when opened, exposed a glistening flight of steps, carved in the stone, and down which the light from their lantern slipped and dripped from flag to flag.

Plainly that stairway had not been used for many a day. It led them to a still lower level. Apparently in the old days, the Vereals had sunk a way deep into the earth and even below the roots of the hill on which their house stood.

Under heavy arches, supported by great rudely squared pillars of the natural stone, through narrow passages, through vast and empty chambers or among vague litters of débris, they came to another corner and Joseph Simon leaned his whole weight against the rock. To the astonishment of the others, what appeared to be the solid stone gave way, and they saw before them a low passage which dipped yet deeper into the earth.

Down this they proceeded, half stifled by the foulness of the long-imprisoned air. They found that the passage turned once or twice at sharp angles, until it opened suddenly into a small room around the sides of which were ranged stout boxes of oak, secured with iron clasps and bands.

Simon, at the sight of these, uttered a cry of joy. Then, as though a second fear presented itself to him, he rushed to the nearest box and raised the cover. The interior was seen piled to the top with black bars and Joseph Simon, dropping upon his knees, cast up his trembling hands in thanksgiving.

Then Silas Denny, with an opened knife gleaming in his hand, stepped forward and scratched one of the black bars. The point of the knife left a glistening mark behind it. That clumsy little chest was piled to the brim with silver bullion. They passed on, now, to the examination of others. By far the greater majority were silver.

But finally they came upon two crowded with purest gold, glimmering and bright as on the day when it had first been placed in this dungeon.

In the farthest corner was a small casket. This Simon himself rushed to the instant he had risen from his knees, and opening it, he broke into half-choked, foolish laughter, dipping his hands into the contents and letting a bright shower of jewels rain back into it—red and green and facets of the most liquid light.

He stopped suddenly; he replaced the casket on the floor and stood stiffly, listening.

"Close everything as it was!" he commanded hoarsely. "Then up through the house again before we're trailed here. Quickly, quickly, my friends!"

When they stood again in the library, Joseph Simon was a man transformed, as though the sight of the treasure had given him new strength. He became, at once, the controlling factor.

"Gentlemen," said Joseph Simon, "you have just seen nearly three million in what is better than cash. We are now to consider how it may safely be taken from San Triste. Who can make a suggestion?"

There was only one, which was to gather the mules and muleteers the next day, arrange the packs, and start for the border.

"Suppose that we have time to do that," said Simon, "we will no sooner have started than José Vereal arrives in San Triste, proves his identity, and at once five hundred well-mounted men take our trail to recover what they will think we have stolen—for this is the curse upon the money, that though it honestly belongs to me, I have no hope under heaven of proving my right to it! We will be overtaken.

"We will be dragged back. The treasure will be lost. We ourselves will be thrown into Mexican prisons until we rot in the damp!"

He paused again. When there was no further suggestion, but only faces dark with thought, he went on firmly: "There is only one way. José Vereal must be intercepted."

"If we knew to what point he was traveling—yes!" said Halsey. "But where is he aimed? How could we know him if we met him!"

"A young man traveling with one of eighty years. That is enough," said Simon calmly. "We can recognize him by that. As for his goal, it has been appointed by Cabrillo— some place which Cabrillo knows very well. With what places is Cabrillo most familiar? With San Triste and his own home.

"He would not have them come near San Triste; there is too much danger here. He has already found that John Jones is dangerous. He would select for the meeting, I am sure, some place near his own home. At some place near his old ranch he has directed Louis Gaspard to meet him. But we, my friends, must meet Vereal and Gaspard first! Consider this!"

He drew a piece of paper from his pocket. Upon it he sketched a hasty map.

"Here lies the ranch among the mountains. To the north there are forty ways of approach. If Vereal and Gaspard come from that direction, we are lost and cannot hold them.

"But if they come from the south—you see? Here is a single pass through the mountains. To that pass we must ride and there we must wait.

"When the two come, they must be encountered. Be sure that they will ride alone. I remember Gaspard well. He loves money too well to waste any of it hiring guards or servants. Here you are—four famous fighters—tell me, my friends, will not Señor Vereal be a fortunate man if he beats you down, all four?"

They looked to one another, the three, smiling faintly, their eyes kindling with a new hope, and behind that hope each saw his share of the three million in "something better than cash!"

"There is only one difficulty," said the Kid, who had been staring down at the floor all this time.

"Ah?" queried Joseph Simon sharply.

"We cannot band against him."

"What!"

"There is to be no murder," said the Kid, still speaking slowly, and fighting his way from word to word. He looked up with a sigh. "If there is a fair fight—that is one thing. If there are three against one, that is plain murder."

Joseph Simon began to laugh and beat his hands together in an ecstasy of rage.

"The devil is talking of fair play!" he cried. "Do you hear this, friends?"

But the three looked steadily at the Kid and seemed to forget that Simon was in the room.

"There's something in what he says," said Halsey. "But, as he remarked, there is nothing wrong with a fair fight. I'll be glad to have the privilege of meeting him first. After that, when he has finished with me, I'll let the rest of you try your hands."

With this, he coughed modestly and made a faint motion toward the armpit under his left shoulder. Hanging there was a holster supporting a neat little instrument of destruction of the smallest and the most effective compass. It threw seven shots in a continuous stream when the finger pressed the trigger. There needed only a steady hand to hold it while it hosed the life out of an enemy with its spray of .45 caliber bullets, and the hand of Halsey was as steady as rock.

So that matter was decided. All four were to start at once for the mountains among which lay the ranch of Cabrillo, and there they were to do their best to waylay the travelers. As for Joseph Simon, he was to remain in the house of the Vereal, where the Kid was to leave instructions for the entertainment of his guest. It needed only that they should depart one by one and by different routes so that they should never be connected all together with this enterprise.

As for the route, Simon laid it out for them with the most particular care. There were many ways by which they could travel. A dozen years before, Gaspard and young José had wandered blindly through the hills for a day and a half before they reached their goal. But seven or eight hours of steady riding would bring one to the spot, if the way were well known.

Therewith the three departed and the Kid went to Vasca Corteño.

"An old servant of my father is now in this house," he said. "Let him be entertained as if my father were still living. I speak of Joseph Simon."

Vasca Corteño bowed. "Señor," he said, "I have seen him and a sad day has come to San Triste again."

After that, the Kid left word that he would be absent for two days or perhaps three, and went out to order his horse. There was no longer any questioning of his decisions in the stable. Since the riding of the brown helding, even Tom Leven seemed to feel that a master had come, at last, who knew horseflesh. Therefore, the black stallion, Pierre, was saddled at once, and soon his long, smooth gallop was driving John Jones across the hills toward the mounains which lay far to the south and west, huge and blue and cold.

23

"One moment of deep and quiet thought," said Louis Gaspard, "is worth all the treasures of the world in gold and diamonds."

"It is true, maestro," said the youth. "Yet," he added

with a sigh, "it is hard to think when one is racked by such a scarecrow of a horse as this!"

Gaspard looked frowningly upon him who knew himself only as Felipe Carvajal, and he thought of what manner of horse his pupil would have bestrode if all that was due him as the true Vereal came into his hands. Then, for the thousandth time, he wondered what might be the meaning of the call from Cabrillo which had summoned him and his pupil toward Mexico.

For, he supposed, if that errand should directly or indirectly result in the exposure to José Vereal of his true ancestry, there might be dire results for him in the mind of José, alias Felipe. He decided, on the spot, to plant an antitoxin against all possible poison in the mind of the young man. Moreover, they were fast drawing toward the mouth of that pass which, eventually, would carry them through the mountains to the north toward the spot which had been appointed as the meeting place by Cabrillo.

"Is a man made," said Gaspard, "who has clothes to wear which are in the fashion?"

"Surely not," said the pupil.

"Is a man happy," continued the teacher, "who has servants, a great house, and much wealth at his disposal?"

"By your teaching, no," said the youth.

"But by yourself, do you doubt it?"

"No," said the young man.

"What, then, is of value?"

"Surely, only a brain which thinks truly and clearly."

"Such a brain, Felipe, it has been the labor of my life to equip you with."

"That was a thousand times kind."

"I have striven," went on the tutor, "to make you a man equipped with the learning of the ages and above all with that fearlessness without which a man, and the best of men, is as nothing. If I have done so much, then I shall flatter myself that there is little more to be done in order to finish."

"Maestro," said the youth, "who am I to criticize? You found me a beggar, and out of your infinite goodness, you have furnished me with food and with clothing; with learning and with behavior. What have I to criticize?''

The teacher, however, could not rest with an answer which had so little of the positive about it.

"I tell you, my son," he went on vigorously, "that if I had seen you about to become heir to millions, I should have prevented it, if possible, in order to take you to myself and make of you this thing that I have succeeded in!"

Felipe nodded and waved a completely assenting and a modest hand.

"Forget what I have said about the horse," he said humbly. "It was merely a passing thought. No doubt, it is by learning to make the best of such a horse as this that I shall finally know how to make the most of a fine animal if it is ever my good fortune to possess one—a horse, for instance, like the one which that fellow yonder is riding!"

It was a dancing chestnut managed by the sure hand of no other than Pierre Gaston Marmont. He swept toward them along a trail which branched across theirs. It was at the crossing that he met the old man and the youth.

"There is a fellow," said Louis Gaspard, "with a gay horse and a reckless manner, but what can you say of the thoughts which are behind his eyes? How rich are his moments of quiet and loneliness?"

Marmont had drawn up the chestnut and, after waving a greeting toward the two, appeared to be busying himself with the contents of a saddlebag.

"In his quiet moments," said young Felipe Carvajal—to give him that adopted name—"in his quiet moments, he can be contented by simply thinking about himself, for I am sure it is a picture worth thought!"

With this he laughed, but the laughter died away when Marmont turned with a tigerish and unreasoning fury upon him.

"Sir, sir!" shouted Marmont. "Do you dare to laugh at me?"

"I crave ten thousand pardons," said Felipe, and he bowed low across the pommel of his saddle to the stranger. "I was not laughing at you, sir."

"At what, then? At what, then?" cried Marmont, advancing threateningly closer to Felipe.

"Be warned, stranger," called Gaspard, grinning with toothless joy. "Be warned and keep off. This is no helpless child with whom you are picking a fight!"

"A young dog who dares to mock a man in the open highway!" thundered Marmont, and with his left hand—for his right was upon the butt of his revolver—he swayed up the quirt to lay it upon the shoulders of the younger man. Exactly what happened, then, Marmont was never afterward exactly sure. But the whip arm was struck by the iron-hard edge of the hand of Felipe, paralyzing every motor nerve in it.

At the same time, driving his spurs into the flanks of his scatter-boned steed, Felipe made the poor brute lunge full at Marmont's fine horse. The chestnut reared; the revolver which Marmont had drawn was dropped into the dust as he clutched the pommel to keep from being unseated; and in the next instant a driving fist clipped him squarely upon the side of the chin.

Darkness rushed over the brain of Marmont. He wakened finally to find that the two were gone; the fine chestnut was gone also; but nearby stood a down-headed, ragged animal which had been bestrode, before the encounter, by honest Louis Gaspard. Tears of rage and humiliation swam into the eyes of Marmont and, kneeling by the side of the horse, he raised his hands and vowed passionately that he would follow this trail to the death.

He mumbled these words from one side of his mouth; for half of his face was as swollen as though he had been struck by the head of a sledgehammer.

"That foolish fellow," said the tutor in the meantime, as he enjoyed the fine paces of the chestnut, which continually had to be checked in order to keep the horse which Felipe rode from falling to the rear, "that foolish fellow will learn to ride better and to fight better before he hunts trouble again."

There was a slight flush in the cheeks of Felipe Carvajal, and his eyes were shining. He was looking hungrily about him, as though he wanted to pass quickly through just such another encounter.

"He was not sure of his weapon," said Felipe quietly. "Otherwise, a bullet would have ended the fight."

"Why did you take the chance? Why did you not draw your own gun, Felipe?"

"I guessed that the quick charge would unsettle him and his horse," said Felipe. "But—do you think we are in the right to have taken his horse?"

"No judge in the land would condemn us," said the old man, patting the silken neck of the chestnut. "We are set upon at a crossroad by one who draws a gun to murder us. We defeat him, and then we take the robber's horse so that we may the more effectually fly from his revenge!"

He laughed loudly at the thought; in his heart he was calculating the price of the animal which they had thus obtained for nothing. Then his thoughts drifted on to a still more pleasant topic. He had seen the mind of Felipe tested in a thousand ways, but he had never before seen him fight, and having seen it, he was contented.

"He is truly a Vereal," said the old man to himself. "He is truly one of the fearless!"

Here the trail twisted around an elbow turn and they came sharply in sight of a wide-shouldered man who was seated upon a magnificent roan—an even finer animal than the chestnut which the tutor was now riding, and in his right hand was a subnosed automatic which was leveled upon young Felipe.

"Gentlemen," said Halsey, for it was he, "I regret that I am forced to stop you. Kindly raise your hands. So!"

They had obeyed in silence, but while the chestnut had halted, the ugly brute on which Felipe rode, pressed forward.

"Halt your horse!" commanded Halsey sharply.

Felipe shouted an order; but his mount still moved on, secretly impelled by the touch of a spur on his right flank.

"The brute is deaf!" cried Felipe to Halsey. "What can I do, señor, while my hands are in the air?"

"Put one on the rein—put the left hand on the rein," said Halsey. "Lower that hand and stop the horse. At your peril, señor!"

The left hand of Felipe, accordingly, was lowered toward

the rein, and it was put down gently, as though the awe of the leveled gun had half frozen his muscles.

Halsey had begun to smile faintly, seeing how completely the game was in his hand. But, at the last instant, the left hand of Felipe leaped out of its slowly descending gesture, whipped a Colt from the holster above his knee, and fired the weapon at the same instant.

So utterly was Halsey taken by surprise and so lightning fast had that movement been, that the trigger of his own leveled gun was not touched. He received the fire point-blank; the bullet tore through his right arm between the elbow and the shoulder, and his weapon fell to the ground. He had no chance to move again to help himself. The wiry arms of Felipe were instantly about him, and he was thrown heavily down among the dried brown grasses. His head struck a stone, and he became unconscious.

He wakened as Marmont had done before him, to find that his roan charger was gone, and in its place stood that clumsy-limbed brute which Felipe had ridden. The two were gone long before. There was not even a dust cloud. Yet they had stayed for one act of mercy. His right sleeve had been slashed away and a rude but very effective bandage had been turned around his wounded arm.

No vows of vengeance fell from the lips of Halsey, but deciding that he would wait for a time until the exquisite pain of his injury had subsided, he moved into the shade of a tree, put his back against the trunk, and lighted a cigarette.

He said quietly at last, through the thick blue-brown cloud of smoke: "I am growing old and foolish. However, perhaps we will meet again!"

Felipe and his tutor, in the meantime, were wheeling down the trail at a round canter. Their two bony nags were now replaced with fine-blooded chargers. They had left behind them two enemies crushed; and Felipe could not help from singing as he rode along. Gaspard, watching him, felt that since the world began, a finer youth had never existed.

They came to the top of a rise and through the bushes on the crest, looking down into the hollow beyond, they saw a third horseman riding toward them, a tall man, as well mounted as either of the other two who had this day interrupted the journey.

"Felipe," said Gaspard, "there is no doubt of it. We have enemies in wait for us. I would swear that that fellow is the third. No doubt that you could master him, but let us not challenge fate. Perhaps after two victories the third encounter would mean defeat."

Felipe sighed. "Alas, maestro," he said, "why should we hide from any man—and upon this lucky day!"

"No words!" snapped out Gaspard. "Follow me!"

He led the way into a thick covert of trees and shrubbery and through this screen they watched Silas Denny ride past them, big, grim of face, formidable, most plainly.

"He is the third, then," said Felipe, as Denny disappeared down the trail. "How many more?"

"Not many," answered Gaspard, and riding again out to the crown of the little rise, he pointed ahead down the valley.

"There," he said, "is the goal of our journey, and nothing can keep us from it now, surely!"

24

The day had worn on to the dusk—a wonderful period when sky and earth were flooded with a steady, rose-tinted light. Gaspard had pointed out a little white-walled hovel far up on the opposite slope of the naked brown mountain. Toward this they now pushed; they dismounted and passed in through the door.

In the meantime, down the pass had stormed Marmont as fast as the wretched nag upon which he was mounted would permit. In due time, he overtook Halsey, in the very act of commencing his return journey, with his right arm supported by a rude sling.

"I have met the devil," said Halsey, smiling, "and the devil won. And you, Marmont?"

"I should have carved him to bits," cried Marmont, "but my horse reared like a light-headed fool at the critical moment, and then—"

"I can see the rest of the story for myself," said Halsey, looking at the swollen side of the face of Marmont.

"You do not understand that—"

"Exactly. It was bad luck. I had equally bad luck. But at least he had to use his gun and not his fist on me. Marmont, be frank. We have both been fairly and squarely thrashed. Confess it!"

The Frenchman groaned, so great was his humiliation and his despair. "It was luck and the rearing of my horse," he said, "but I shall meet him again."

"I hope to have that privilege," said Halsey. "But perhaps it would be better for both of us if we failed. He is a young tiger, Marmont!"

"I'll cut the claws of that tiger!" cried Marmont.

They went on down the trail, relating in details their experiences until there hove before them as they rounded a turn of the trail, no other than big Silas Denny on a sweating horse. They greeted him with shouts; but they learned at once that he, at the least, had not been a victim of this true Vereal. Perhaps he was even worse, for he had been completely dodged.

"We have gone hunting rabbits and we have beat up a lion," said Halsey, summing it up. "Marmont and I have been shamefully outwitted and outfought; and you, Denny, have been completely given the slip. We have been little better than three fools, and I tell you both, very frankly, that I would trade my share of the three million in La Casa Vereal, for a ticket to New Orleans, and call it a mighty lucky trade !"

"We are still two men and a half," cried Marmont. "In the name of all that is great, let us go back down the valley as fast as we may and see if we may not overtake them."

"Mounted on such horses?" said Halsey.

Marmont groaned, but Denny urged that they go forward even as Marmont had suggested. "There's one chance in a hundred. But a hundredth part of a chance for three million is worth taking," as Denny put it.

So they rode on down the pass until, in the thick of the evening, they came in view of a white-walled hut up the naked side of the mountain. They found themselves now in darkness, upon unfamiliar ground, and they decided that it would be manifest folly to push on blindly through the night. Far better to go to this little house. If it were unoccupied, at least it would afford them shelter. If it were occupied, they would be hospitably received.

They were halfway from the trail to this house when they heard a sound which assured them that the place was indeed not without a tenant. It was a man's voice accompanied by a guitar, a ringing, rather high-pitched voice, and the song was conducted with a free-swinging abandon which told of some art and more high spirits.

"I tell you there is liquor in that house," said Halsey, moistening his dry lips, and he pushed his horse ahead at a rounder pace. He had not uttered a syllable of complaint on account of his wound, but the thought of a drink now made him almost fierce with expectation. The others followed him in all haste, but when they came close to the house they dismounted and approached the open door with some caution.

Flames were rolling and roaring on an open hearth, throwing light on all within the house, which consisted of a single room. In three corners of it sat three men, cross-legged upon the hard-packed dirt floor, their ankles and their hands tied with bits of rope.

They were Cabrillo, Louis Gaspard, and the true Vereal, whose third adventure on this day had been unfortunate indeed, for a red-stained bandage was coiled about his head. In front of the fire, sitting cross-legged also and facing the others, was the singer, the guitar upon his lap and his head raised to give full voice to a high note. It was John Jones, alias the Kid!

So stunned were the three beholders that they could not

speak or move until the song ended, and then they broke through the doorway with a shout of triumph. The Kid did not rise to greet them. He merely contented himself with thrumming his fingers across the strings of the guitar once or twice, while he smiled up at the newcomers.

"All the luck has run out of my hands," said the Frenchman, almost more bitterly than happily, "and into the hands of the youngster. The devil is in it!"

"Jones," said Silas Denny, "you've made all four of us with this turn!"

But Halsey said nothing at all. He detached himself from the group, as he so often would do, and regarded the others as though they made a picture which had nothing to do with himself or his fortunes, his forehead wrinkling as he looked at them.

"Now," said Halsey at last, "what's to be done with 'em?"

The Kid rose, and with his three coadjutors withdrew toward the doorway where they conferred in low voices as to the fate of the prisoners. These, although they could hear no more than a word now and then, could easily guess that life and death depended upon this whispered conference.

"Dead men," said Silas Denny, "do no talking."

"That is true," murmured Marmont.

"Would you kill them in cold blood?" asked Halsey.

"No—in hot blood," answered Marmont. "Suppose that the fire should catch—"

He did not complete the sentence except with a shrug of the shoulders, and all four turned involuntarily with looks of horror or of pity to the three captives. The latter could well understand by those looks what had been proposed. Cabrillo turned a dirty yellow. His eyes rolled wildly and his mouth sagged open. He was like a cornered wild beast.

Old Gaspard looked at his pupil with a faint groan, as though he saw the work of the past dozen years wiped out by a single blow, and all his hopes with it, caring nothing, however, for his own life. Only José Vereal kept a dauntless countenance. He had understood as well as the others, but he looked without flinching into the faces of the three.

Then the Kid gave his vote. "If there is a slaughter," he said, "you'll have to get rid of four men, not three. I'll be the fourth!"

"Look here, lad," said Si Denny persuasively. "You've done a tidy bit of work today. However things turn out, if we win in the end, your share will be the largest of the lot. Do you want to throw away everything that you've won for us?"

Then Halsey broke in: "He's right. I say this: Let me stay here with them. My bad arm makes me very little use in a pinch. Marmont can stay with me. You and Denny, Jones, go back to San Triste. Push through everything as fast as you can. Three days ought to be enough. At the end of three days, Marmont and I will break away and start to join you. Then let these fellows cut through their ropes as fast as they can. We'll take our chance against them."

"We'd be overtaken before we got to the river," said Denny emphatically. "We could never get to the border, driving a train of seventy mules."

"There's a better thing to do than that," suggested Halsey. "There's a little tramp freighter in port at Ulloa. Even with mules at a walk you can make Ulloa; make a bargain to buy that little ship. It's the *Rachel* from New Orleans.

"She has a burden of three hundred tons only, but she's as fast as a yacht. You can buy her for a song. Very well, at the end of three days, unless we hear from you to the contrary, we leave these where they are and drive away for Ulloa. By the time we get there, you'll be aboard with steam up, ready to shoot away to sea."

"Look," broke in Marmont to the Kid, laying a persuasive hand upon his shoulder, "one bullet will finish the real Vereal and give you the whole estate forever without any question. Are you going to be a fool, like Halsey?"

The Kid thought not, be it said to his credit, of all the huge wealth of the Vereal which was now indeed within his grip, but he saw once more the loveliness of Alicia de Alvarado, and his heart grew big in his breast. If ever the devil, then, came into the face of a man, it was in the face of the Kid, so that he turned and cast one glance of fire toward young José. But the latter met that terrible gaze with a steady eye. For a single instant they looked squarely at each other, and then the conquered became the conqueror and the Kid turned back to his three companions.

"Marmont," he muttered hoarsely, "you are the devil—not a man! But the Vereal is not to be touched. That's flat and final. Since the luck turned against him, he hasn't uttered a single whisper of complaint. He's a man!"

Denny and Marmont groaned, but Halsey nodded in affirmation of this position. He had been standing back a little from the others while they conferred, and now he was looking shrewdly from one to another—from the false Vereal to the true one. They might easily have passed for brothers, so great was their resemblance to each other. The jaw of the Kid was a little more square and his forehead a trifle wider and loftier. Those were the only differences of importance. For the rest, in body and feature they were of one type.

Silas Denny made a gesture of resignation, and he summed up the whole matter in a single sentence: "Jones," he said, "you've given away five million!"

25

The telegraph office in San Triste was hardly opened the next morning before Silas Denny was busy. His first message was to the steamer *Rachel*, in the port of Ulloa, and it read: "Captain of the ship *Rachel*, Ulloa. Desire to engage *Rachel* for one month, reply stating terms. Silas Denny, Hotel Republica, San Triste."

It was an empty wire to the little town of Ulloa that morning, and the reply came back almost at once:

"*Rachel* busy. (Signed) Captain Macpherson."

When he had read this, Denny shrugged his wide shoulders.

"A Scotchman," he said to himself. "This will be a hard bargain to drive!"

He wired again:

"Will offer a thousand above your present contract price for the *Rachel* for one month."

Then he waited eagerly and finally received the terse word: "Not enough."

Macpherson, apparently, was not unwilling to break his contract, after all, but he had smelled a rat.

Denny wired again: "Will make offer two thousand."

The reply came back swiftly. Evidently Captain MacPherson was lingering at the telegraph office in Ulloa until this odd bargain was struck.

"My price ten thousand."

"Five thousand," answered Denny, groaning at the thought of such a price.

"Good-by," came the answer of Macpherson.

"Ten thousand it is," wired Denny. "Cash on sight in advance."

"Waiting orders," came the pleasant response of Macpherson.

"Victual ship, get steam up for quick start," answered Denny.

Then this final shrewd word came from Macpherson. "I thought so."

"He thinks too darned much!" muttered Denny, as he walked from the office in the cool of the evening through the streets of San Triste. He went straight up the hill to La Casa Vereal.

There had been much bustling around La Casa Vereal all that day. The Kid had given his orders, and from various of the Vereal farms near San Triste and from the hills adjoining, thirty fine Spanish mules were being collected. For it had been decided at the last moment that it was foolish to consider moving the great bulk of the treasure, which was silver. It composed not one tenth part of the value of the whole mass, though in bulk it was three quarters.

While they would need more than seventy mules to carry the entire weight of all that Joseph Simon had assembled those dozen years before in that secret room underground, it was estimated, when he and the Kid, with the assistance of a scales, laid out the gold in mule loads, that twenty-two mules would be enough to carry the burden.

The extra eight animals which were being assembled would merely serve to lighten the loads in order that faster time might be made on the trip to Ulloa, while if an accident happened to any of the carriers, the precious load could be shifted to one of the few spare units in the little caravan.

This was only part of the necessary preparation. The next was to select a dozen stout peons, picked men of their class, who would be able to conduct the mules to Ulloa and, once there, assist in the rapid shifting of the cargo to the *Rachel* at the pier. The dozen could not be easily found.

To be sure, there were many stout fellows near San Triste, but what Joseph Simon needed for this work were men who would be willing to take their lives in their hands for the sake of a doubled or tripled fee. By the end of the first day, only four had been gathered whom he considered of the correct type.

But, by this time, the mules had arrived, the *Rachel* was known to be waiting at their service in the little port of Ulloa, and the second day could be spent solely in assembling the remaining eight or ten muleteers who were needed, in loading the animals and in the start.

That start was made in the mid-afternoon. Two tons and fifteen hundred weight of gold dust had been emptied by Simon and the Kid with their own hands into little bags of the stoutest canvas, each bag containing fifty pounds. So divided, it would not only be possible to arrange the weights on the packsaddles to the best advantage, but also the unloading of the train at the pier might be conducted with the greatest possible expedition.

By the Kid and Joseph Simon, too, those bags had been carried from the secret chamber up the incline to the room above. The Kid had seen Simon lean against the wall with a hand pressed against his eyes, sick at heart, as he took his last glimpse of the silver which they must leave behind them on that forced march to the sea. Then both retired; the heavy door was turned back into its place in the wall, and the

muleteers were brought down into the bowels of La Casa
Vereal to carry up the loads for the mules.

It was inevitable that they should guess what was happening.
There is only one probable thing which is as weighty as lead,
or even weightier, and yet which is as soft as sand. Before
half a dozen of those sacks had been handled a swift, almost
frightened whisper had passed among the muleteers: "Gold!"
Another added, seeing Joseph Simon hanging anxiously in
the distance: "Gold for Simon."

News of murder travels no faster than tidings of treasure.
In some mysterious manner the rumor passed through La
Casa Vereal. Twenty mules, loaded with gold for Joseph
Simon, were about to leave La Casa Vereal.

It was the very thing which Simon most wished to avoid.
For that purpose he had ordered that the mules and the
muleteers be assembled, the pack saddles in readiness, and
then only as a last step the little sacks would be loaded on and
the whole caravan start hurriedly off toward the sea. But
before the head of the first mule was led out onto the
highway, the story was burning its way through San Triste.

"Simon has La Casa Vereal in his clutches again!" said
men and women to one another, and they shook their heads.
"Better a Cabrillo in the house on the hill than a Joseph
Simon. Now we will all be ground underfoot once more!"

Lest just such a rumor should start, Simon would have
taken the strongest possible guard with the caravan, but Silas
Denny retorted that a strong guard would be just strong
enough to hold them up and rob them. Accordingly, with no
more dispute, they agreed upon the final details.

The thirty miles to Ulloa could be traversed by the mules,
even allowing for sufficient halts to rest them, and even
having due regard for the roughness of the mountainous way,
in fifteen hours or less. Since they left San Triste at four in
the afternoon, they might expect that an all-night march
would bring them into Ulloa by seven the next morning, at
the latest. Once there, the plan was of course to shift the
treasure on board the *Rachel* as soon as possible.

That the *Rachel* was waiting for them, there could be no
doubt. A wire had come to Denny from Macpherson that day:

"Do you need special crew?" Denny had thought it wise to wire back: "Any crew will suit. Work simple."

"Otherwise," he had explained to Joseph Simon, "this Macpherson, who seems to be a canny Scot, may have a fine gang of thugs ready to take advantage of chances."

If all worked out as they hoped it would work, they would be in Ulloa a full day earlier than Halsey and Marmont had reason to expect. Presumably, the second half of their party would scurry across the hills the night which followed the morning of their arrival at Ulloa. When they arrived, steam would long since have been up on the ship, and they would be ready to dart away to sea as fast as possible.

Once out to sea, if the wily Macpherson had any thought of setting hand on the cargo, he would be deterred by the guns of four practiced fighters. For the Kid, who of course had to stay behind in San Triste, less any rank suspicion should grow up, was to leave La Casa Vereal something after midnight of the second day and rush for Ulloa.

Simon stated the great objection to the whole scheme. "There are too many people who have to do things separately and yet meet at one point at one time. It will never be done, my young friends."

"There'd be no need of trouble," said Denny gloomily. "We could all of us have settled down in San Triste and lived like kings. But the Kid got an attack of conscience at the last minute. He couldn't see his way clear to getting rid of this young rat—Vereal!"

But he and Simon stared without kindness upon the Kid, but the latter paid them no heed. He had hardly made a comment upon the whole scheme since he returned to La Casa Vereal with Silas Denny. He had helped faithfully in the work of preparing the mule train and the sacking of the gold. But aside from that, he was of no use to them.

So, at the last moment, when Simon and Denny were about to mount their horses and start off with the train, the former could not help saying to John Jones: "One would think that you were not in this business, Mr. Jones! I hired your brain as well as your hands, young man!"

The response was astonishing. A red fury glittered in the

eyes of the Kid, and he broke out: "Damn you and your hire and Denny and the rest. I see this through because I started it, but I wish to heaven that I'd never seen your faces!"

They recoiled from him then as though he had held a gun in their faces, and it was not until the bells of the mules were jingling far down the slope that Denny spoke again.

"Marmont was right," he said. "When a man seems to go off his head for no reason, it's ten to one that there's some woman behind it!"

26

The first day of captivity went easily enough for Cabrillo and his two companions. They were given what liberty could be expected. Food was provided by the old shepherd to whom the hut belonged. When he returned to his house and found it filled with strangers, a bit of money had passed into his hand from Halsey, and that had been enough to buy him body and soul.

With a source of supplies guaranteed in this fashion, Marmont and Halsey had no mind to be too severe with their prisoners. The three were hobbled and permitted to walk back and forth near the shack, though their hands were constantly secured, while Marmont or Halsey, or both, sat nearby with a naked gun ready in case of an attempt to escape.

Halsey had told the three, frankly enough, that they were in no danger. They would be confined there for a few days only, and after that, they could go; but Cabrillo and the others had another mind about the matter. They could not look upon that handsome young angel of wrath, Pierre Marmont, without the greatest misgivings.

Plainly he did not wish to see them regain their liberty, and he was now the dominating factor, simply because Halsey was half crippled by his wound. It was a clean flesh wound, to be sure, and it was rapidly righting itself, but nevertheless he was only half a man if matters should come to a decision. He could not keep Marmont from doing as the latter pleased in the last analysis.

This was what Cabrillo announced to his companions as they walked back and forth in front of the hut in the hot sun of this afternoon—at the very time, indeed, when the mule train was beginning to jingle its way down the hill from San Triste. Gaspard agreed. As for Felipe Carvajal, he did not express an opinion, for he had been taught by his tutor that a young man should not push himself forward.

"Señor Vereal!" called Marmont from the doorway of the hut, where he sat with a rifle across his knees, on guard.

At that call, Felipe started and looked wildly around him. Twelve years of a new name and a new life had by no means blotted out of his mind all that had passed before. He stared at Gaspard, and then toward Marmont.

"To whom does he speak?" muttered Felipe.

Gapard had grown very pale. He saw the blow about to fall, and he was weak with fear.

"You, señor!" repeated Marmont harshly, pointing.

"Do you speak to me?" asked the youth.

"I do!"

"My name, señor, is Felipe Carvajal."

"It is now. It was once another thing. It was once José Vereal."

Felipe looked to Gaspard, alarmed. He had been raised to believe that the name of Vereal could not be mentioned without danger in Mexico.

"But," cried Marmont, "is it possible that you have not yet heard the whole truth? By the heavens, it is a pretty story, and the two rascals haven't told it to you yet? They'd have let you die without learning the truth of their villainy!" He studied the strained faces of the pair and broke into joyous laughter, for he loved cruelty.

"Look at them, Vereal!" he commanded.

Felipe, or to give him his right name, José, looked earnestly at his tutor, and he saw there enough guilt and misery to make him blush in turn.

"This rascal Cabrillo," said Marmont, "bought up your tutor. You could have stepped into the estate a dozen years ago with no one to raise a hand against you. But Cabrillo found the price of Gaspard and he's kept him on salary ever since. That is why you have had another name, though how the devil Gaspard could have made you think that a new name was necessary, I can't make out. There's the story in a nutshell. Now thank Gaspard for what he's done! I've heard you call him your benefactor!"

He leaned forward, grinning expectantly, and José turned with an exclamation of horror to Gaspard. There was no need for the latter to confess. His head had fallen upon his chest. A fast pulse beat in his sunken temples.

Whatever revulsion of feeling passed through the mind of the younger man, he mastered it swiftly. He went to Gaspard and with his bound hands took the withered fingers of the old man.

"Maestro," he said, "look up and feel no shame."

"Ah, José," groaned Gaspard, "trample me under your feet; load me with curses. I have done a damnable thing. I have betrayed a helpless child!"

"No, no!" said José. "Do you think that I have forgotten, maestro, how the bullet struck me down and how you raised me and carried me away? Having saved my life, it was yours to do with as you chose. What you chose to do with it, I shall never blame you for."

The shame, the joy, the relief of the old man found a vent in the tears that began to run down his cheeks. "Ah, José," he murmured, "to be forgiven is more terrible than to be denounced."

Marmont, in the meantime, had stared at the pair with an amazement which was almost horror. He rubbed his hand across his eyes once or twice in bewilderment; then he looked again and made sure that he had not dreamed this astonishing thing. For his own part, forgiveness was not in his nature.

"And Cabrillo?" he asked sharply. "Is he forgiven likewise?"

"I have not asked for it," said Cabrillo sullenly. "But at

least it was I who called you back to return your estate to you, José. Remember that!''

"When another man had driven you out, Cabrillo!" put in Marmont.

"Sir," said José to Cabrillo, "I have neither the wish nor the right to judge you hastily. There will be time for that hereafter."

There was such a noble simplicity in his voice and his manner that Cabrillo could make no audible word in his muttered reply. As for Marmont, he relieved his feelings with a curse or two and then called to Halsey, and when the latter came, they began a low-voiced conference.

The three prisoners, continuing their walk slowly up and down before the house, could hear Halsey protesting—could hear Marmont affirming with a greater and greater vehemence.

"He is maddened," said Gaspard, "by finding that you are not a savage like himself. Unless God intervenes to help us, I fear that our last hour is coming fast upon us, friends! But oh, José, I praise God that you have learned the truth before the end, and that you have forgiven me in spite of it!"

"That maundering can be left out, old man," said Cabrillo. "What is important is the first part of what you say. I can see that devil out of the corner of my eye, handling his rifle. Let us go inside. There is nothing that can be done while we are here. Let us go into the house, and if the time comes, at least we will throw ourselves on them and fight with our bound hands!"

So said Cabrillo, softly, but with the determination of one whose life is worth only a small purchase. The others, since they could see nothing better for it, followed him back into the house.

There was a fire burning under a soup kettle caked with soot, and José picked up the small iron rod which served as a poker. He began to stab at the blazing wood as men do when they are deepest in thought, for it is then that a fire is the most fascinating. He handled the long iron clumsily, for his wrists were bound so closely together that the flow of blood into his fingers had been half stopped.

Now that he had come to the land of his birth he was

snared and perhaps about to be destroyed. There could be little doubt of that prophetic thought. Halsey and Marmont had drawn back from the doorway. Their voices were raised in sharp dispute.

"Then, by heaven," cried Marmont, "I'll do it by myself!"

José could sense his death warrant in the tone of the Frenchman. Yet nothing could be done. He stabbed gloomily at the wood again and as he did so, he saw that the end of the poker, which had lain among the hot coals during his long moment of thought, had become a dull red. Marmont came swiftly into the doorway, rifle in hand, calling over his shoulder: "If we wait too long, that fox, Simon, will be off and leave us behind him. Denny would favor that, too! I know them, I tell you."

Halsey, running after him, caught him by the shoulder and drew him back. They could hear the voice of the Englishman speaking rapidly, desperately, but Louis Gaspard, who knew the English tongue, now sank upon his knees.

"My friends," he murmured, "we are about to die. José, my child, commend yourself to God with your last breath. Tell me—"

His trembling voice died away, for he saw José take from the fire the iron rod with a point now brightest red and throwing off tiny sparks. José motioned to Cabrillo. That one gesture was enough to make the big man understand, and with a gasp of hope, Cabrillo stepped closer and held out his hands. Where the cord twisted between the wrists, José laid the red end of the iron. Instantly a thin column of smoke grew up. Over it leaned Cabrillo and fanned the smoke with his powerful breath until it grew into a thick cloud.

There was a slight snapping sound, another, and Cabrillo's hands separated, the tangle of cord dropping to the floor. There was no word spoken. Marmont was approaching the door, dragging Halsey with him; opposition had driven him to a red frenzy of anger. Cabrillo reached the side of the room with one long, gliding step. From the holster which hung high on a peg he jerked the revolver.

He turned to José and pressed the muzzle of the gun against the twining cords. At the explosion of the Colt, the cords were shorn in two, and as Marmont with a yell of alarm leaped into the doorway, he was in time to see José, also, catch up a gun.

There were two armed men within, two desperate fighters, the prowess of one of whom Marmont had already tasted. Upon his own side there was only himself armed with a rifle, which was a poor weapon for such close work; and behind him was Halsey—only half a man now that he had been wounded.

All of those thoughts thronged through the mind of Marmont during the split part of the second during which he glanced through the doorway. Then he leaped back in time to escape the bullet which Cabrillo fired. That slug spattered into the dobe on the other side of the door. Marmont was already around the corner of the building, with Halsey at his heels.

There was no time for words. Luckily for the pair, they had kept the two best horses constantly saddled, in readiness for any emergency. They threw themselves into the saddles and spurred away, flattened above the reaching necks of the horses. Down the steep slope they flew like arrows off the string.

Cabrillo, in the meantime, had rushed to the front of the hut. Had he thought of the rifle which Marmont had dropped, the flight of the two would not have lasted long, but in the blindness of his joy at this sudden victory, he blazed away with his revolver until it was empty.

He cast that gun away with a thick-throated cry, at last, and caught up the rifle. But the pair were already almost at the bottom of the slope. Even so, he steadied the long barrel and drew his bead. His finger had already curled upon the trigger when a hand knocked the rifle to one side and it exploded with the muzzle harmlessly high in the air.

Cabrillo looked up into the face of José Vereal.

"One of the two," said Vereal, "has been a friend to us when we most needed one. You cannot risk striking him down with your fire!"

27

They rode all three together, Cabrillo and the tutor and Vereal. Surely it seemed strange that the cause of Cabrillo should be the same as that of the man whom he had so bitterly wronged, but he wished, now, for one thing only, and that was to beat down all together, the Kid, and his three compatriots. For that purpose, therefore, his heart and soul were at the service of the true Vereal.

They made their plans as they galloped. They would pause at Cabrillo's ranch, change their horses for fresh ones, and then rush across the hills to get to San Triste as early as possible. At Cabrillo's ranch they would pick up only two or three chosen men—real fighting hands.

It was in San Triste that they must hope to enlarge their force by revealing José and establishing him through the testimony of old Gaspard, no matter how that testimony shamed the tutor. Speed and more speed and still more speed was their requisite, for in the meantime Marmont and Halsey were plunging through the night to get to San Triste, and they would carry the warning with them.

At least, such was the opinion of the three. They could not know that the two fugitives were aiming at Ulloa. But even had San Triste been their goal, Cabrillo felt that they could be overtaken, for he knew the trails between his ranch and San Triste, and he could save many miles by following the correct path.

At Cabrillo's ranch, therefore, they made only a five-minute halt, received new horses, a mouthful of brandy, and galloped away again with only three of Cabrillo's retainers behind them. But the rancher left word that all of his available men should be gathered as soon as possible, and as many more drummed up as would join for the sake of money or a night's adventure.

It was a squadron of six, now, that bore across the hills. For four hours they pushed relentlessly ahead through the late afternoon, through the bright evening, and saw the mountains turn from blue and rose to black. Still they drove ahead down wandering trails or even over unmarked stretches, for Cabrillo, true to his promise, was cutting many a mile from the total length of their journey by leading them over shortcuts, one after the other.

In the midst of one of these breaks across hills which were crossed by no trail, from among the stiff-standing Spanish daggers before them, horsemen started out. Cabrillo and the little party drew up with shouts of dismay and swung to the right. More horsemen defiled before them. They turned to head back, but another group came down behind them to block that way. They had ridden, in short, squarely into a trap which was now sealed before them upon all sides. Before they could prepare for action the wild, Indian yell of the bandits rose from twenty throats: "Grenacho!"

Cabrillo's three men were completely paralyzed by that war cry. They huddled together with wails of terror. Cabrillo himself was little better. Only two men in the party retained some spark of steadiness and courage. Gaspard was one, and José Vereal was the other.

"José!" said the old man, swinging his horse sharply in by the side of the Vereal. "You can remember the name of Grenacho out of your boyhood!"

"Like a nightmare," said José. "He is a murderer and a robber. Is he not?"

"He is. But also, he owed his life to your father. Grenacho is not an ungrateful dog. He will remember. Call out for him, José, and make yourself known to him!"

The outlaws, in the meantime, had rapidly closed in around their victims, their guns glimmering in the pale of the moonlight which seeped through a mist of high-lying clouds. There was no question of resistance. At the first challenge, the hands of José's party went stiffly into the air, but José himself, while he kept his hands carefully raised, urged his horse into the lead.

"Grenacho!" he called. "Is Grenacho among you?"

"Here," answered a deep voice. "Who calls Grenacho?"

He saw riding toward him a powerful man whose size made the tough little mustang on which he was mounted seem like a mere pony. He came closer, until beneath the thick shadow which fell under the brim of the wide sombrero, José could make out sordid, brutal features.

"Are you," said José, "Grenacho?"

"I am. Who are you you, señor?"

"One who will find a friend in you."

Grenacho laughed. "I am the friend of all travelers who ride good horses and carry wallets. I stop them on the road for the sake of a little pleasant talk. What is your name, amigo?"

"José Vereal."

Grenacho uttered an exclamation. "It is a lie," he said. "José Vereal is sleeping soundly in San Triste after sending Simon away. You are a bold man, señor, but you see that I am informed."

"The man you call Vereal," said José, "is a pretender."

"San Triste will die for him, then," said Grenacho. "Come, señor, I like a good bold lie as well as any man. But you have said enough and too much. You must know, then he who calls the Vereal liar, calls me the same!"

"I carry my proof with me," said José quietly.

"I am no scholar to read," answered Grenacho.

"There are no papers to read. There are only men to listen to. You will tell me, Grenacho, who was at the side of José twelve years ago when La Casa Vereal was attacked?"

"The whole world knows. It was the old Frenchman."

"Did you know his face?"

"As my own."

"Gaspard!" called José.

The tutor rode slowly forward.

"Take off your hat, maestro, and let the moon fall on your face."

It was done, and Gaspard raised his age-thinned features to the sky. There was a stifled cry from Grenacho.

"*Madre de Dios!*" he exclaimed. "The dead live again and walk. It is Gaspard!"

"Will his word have weight with you Grenacho?"

"Unless I am a fool. But this is a dream. Gaspard died twelve years ago! And yet this is he!"

"Tell him," commanded José.

The tutor, simply and quietly, told the story. When he was ended, Grenacho crossed himself.

"May the good Lord make my mind clear," he said. "If this is another trick, there will be dead men before the morning comes. But—let me see your face, señor!"

José removed his sombrero. He exposed the thin features and the quiet smile of one sure of himself and his cause. Grenacho had spurred his horse close, but he needed only one glance to make him cry out: "El Vereal!"

He was echoed by a murmur from his men, who had held back from the prey until the leader gave the word. They were obedient.

"Do you believe me?" asked José.

"Is it your brother, or a ghost that lives in La Casa Vereal?"

"An impostor, Grenacho."

"He has taught San Triste to love him, señor. My brain whirls!"

"He is a brave and a wise men, Grenacho. I have already met him!" He raised his hand to the bandage around his head as he spoke.

"Did he leave you free to ride where you wished?"

"He left me under a guard. By the grace of God and good fortune, we have escaped—all three of us have escaped. I admit his courage. I admit that there is danger in attacking him. That is why, Grenacho, I am glad that I have met you. For my father's sake, you will ride with me to San Triste tonight!"

"I shall," cried Grenacho. "We will ride together, my men and I, and if there is fighting, you will see what Grenacho and those who follow Grenacho can do. Lead on, señor. I shall give a word of the truth to my men. Then you will hear them shout like wolves on a trail in winter!

"Ride on! We must take the man in La Casa Vereal first. Afterward, there is to be recovered the treasure which he sent away today with Simon. Ten thousand devils! Had I but known that it was not the money of the true Vereal—"

"However much it may be, it is yours to the last peso,

Grenacho, if you help me back to my house in San Triste and to what is mine by the law!"

There was a hoarse shout of exultation from the outlaw. He whirled his horse. His call gathered his men with a sudden rush about him, and as José rode on, followed by Gaspard and the others, they could hear the great voice of Grenacho thundering behind them, making such a speech as his men could understand.

There was no doubt as to the feeling of those men for the Vereal. The end of Grenacho's speech was answered with a shrill yell which was all and more than the outlaw had promised José. It made the blood of the latter run cold. It was, indeed, like the wail of the wolf pack when it sights the kill.

Now, as they pressed ahead through the hills, the whole band of the outlaws poured in behind them.

28

The daughter of Alvarado woke suddenly and lay in her bed with her pulses beating fast in her temples, for of late she had been sleeping very lightly and tonight when her eyes opened, her mind was not half dimmed with sleep, but she was instantly alert to all that had wakened her.

There had been the treading of many horses; there had been a cessation of that noise, and the stopping of it waked her. Far smaller things could waken her in the past few nights since that evening when her father had said coldly, but quietly, "She shall marry the man to whom her faith has been given; she shall marry Cabrillo or die a virgin. God help me to keep this vow! As for this recent fancy of hers—it must be forgotten!"

Since he had spoken this, with the voice and with the manner of one pronouncing fate itself, a great quiet had fallen even upon the peaceful life of Alicia; and a silence had passed through her heart.

Now she slipped out of bed, put her feet in the warm slippers, and crossed the floor to the window. The wall was so deep that she could not look down to the street. She had to kneel in the casement, and then she could see the very picture that had crossed her mind in her sleep. It was a thing of nameless dread.

Far down the street they were ranged, two and two, or in straggling ranks of threes and fours, the horses with their heads turning restlessly, but their feet never stirring, the vaqueros with not even their heads moving, but with their faces fixed straight forward, full of a purpose, waiting for a signal.

What was to happen?

Then a hand struck against the gate which, every night, closed the archway which led from the street into the patio of her father's house. She heard the night porter drawling sleepily, yet with a faint note of fear in his voice: "Who goes?"

Then a hoarse, deep voice answered: "Where is Federico de Alvarado?"

"Asleep, where all law-keeping folk should be at midnight!"

"Impertinent rat!" called the voice in the street. "Open at once, before I blow the lock off the door. Open at once, I say!"

There was danger, then, indeed, and unlike those sudden wakenings of other nights, this had been a true prophecy of fear. She grew quieter. Her hand ceased shaking and going back to the little dressing chamber which opened off the bedroom, she dressed herself swiftly.

She found herself almost happy in the unknown cause of this coming which had brought the many horsemen into the street, for now her thoughts turned away from herself and dwelt on what calamity that might be hanging over the heads of those she loved in that house. For she loved them dearly— even that hardminded, practical mother—even the cold sternness of her father.

She was dressed at last. She opened the door of her room. There was the beginning of a stir within the house. Others had heard that summons from the street, perhaps. Others were dressing, or listening, as she was doing.

Then, suddenly, she heard the grave voice of her father, saying: "This way, my friends. I shall hear what you have to say, trust me in that!"

She slipped out into the corridor. Down the blackness of the stairs she found a way, until she crouched on a lower step, looking through the yawning door of the library. There were a dozen armed men in there, and there was her father, dressed. No doubt he had not been in bed when the summons came, for he kept late hours among his books.

The lights cleared and burned more brightly with yellow glowing. She could see the rough, unshaven faces. And there was one slender, youthful figure at the first sight of which her heart leaped wildly. Even when he turned, for a moment she doubted still, so very like they were; but then she saw that it was not he from La Casa Vereal.

It was only another with a face most similar and with the same light carriage of the body, a sort of tiptoe grace. Yet there was a difference. He whose face she knew so well had a greater sternness of profile, a nobler forehead, and there were hints of a more supple power about his arms and shoulders.

A very old man stepped forward. He was either sick or else very weary. For the young man helped him gently to a chair.

"This is the man who will give you the proof, señor," said the youth.

"He seems a worthy gentleman," said her father without emotion. "I am only surprised to find him with such a company."

He looked coldly, deliberately about him upon the bearded ruffians. There was a savage murmur among them, but they did nothing.

"My name," said the ancient man, "is one which the señor may have heard many years ago—and yet it is not so very long! I am called Louis Gaspard."

"Louis Gaspard!" murmured her father. Then he shook his head. "I do not recall that name."

"Consider again, señor. I have often seen you in La Casa Vereal in other days, and you have often seen me."

"Ah?" said Alvarado, and now he leaned forward and began to study the face of the old man. "Yes, señor, I have seen you before, and I find that even these many years have not so greatly changed you. That name again?"

"It is Louis Gaspard."

"By heavens!" said Alvarado. "You were the tutor to young José who disappeared on the same night that swept the boy away from San Triste. Is it not so?"

"It is, señor."

"Then, at last, we are to have the truth. Did he live? Did he die in the storming of the house?"

The old man bowed his head; Alicia could see his breast heave with his emotion. But he began to speak at last, a strange, strange story which as she heard she herself could hardly have given credence to, until she saw strange conviction and perfect surety in the face of her father. In the end, he leaped from his chair and cried: "And this man, Gaspard?"

He was pointing to that young man who was so like that other whom she knew so well.

"It is he," said Louis Gaspard. "It is José Vereal!"

What her father did, she could not see. For blankness was drawn across her eyes. When she wakened, she felt that an age had passed; but it was only a second and still her heart was thundering forth that message in her ear: "Your Vereal has been a liar, a traitor, and a knave. He has deceived you in this, as in his love also, doubtless."

She could not rise. She saw a burly ruffian, middle-aged, with the same gruff voice which had given the summons at the gate of the house, put a hand upon the shoulder of Federico de Alvarado and confer with him.

"First," said her father with decision, "we must go to La Casa Vereal. There we will end the pretender with a bullet. Then we will ride out to recover the treasure which, we are reasonably sure, the robber had sent out with Simon. Let us make all haste."

"This is very true. This is clear talk and strong talk," said the burly fellow beside him, "but there are other things to be considered, I pray you! We may ride into a nest of hornets at La Casa Vereal. This pretender is a hero and a fighter. Let us gather help. There are many true men who will instantly rise if you summon them, Señor Alvarado. Let us have their help in this work! You, Cabrillo, can help us also!''

Cabrillo! The name was like a knife stroke, piercing her. There she saw his brutal face, his swaggering, thick shoulders. She stood up, given strength by that touch of horror. Yet, the moment she rose, she knew that she could not go back to her room. All that wave of dangerous fighting men with her very father to head them was to wash up the hill to the Casa Vereal and strike at the life of the nameless man who had said he loved her.

An immense weakness of pity swept over her. It was not love, she told herself, for surely she was wise enough to hate a traitor, who had been shown clearly to her. Yet she could clearly see only two things. One was the face which had leaned close to hers in the Plaza Municipal. The other was the broad-jowled countenance of Cabrillo.

She slipped down the stairs and into the patio. Then she hurried back to the outbuildings—to the stable. In the box stall she found her red-bay mare, Julietta. She nosed her mistress with a velvet muzzle and a soft whinny, and Alicia saddled her quickly, bridled her, and led her through the side door of the stable. It opened onto the street. She mounted, and at once the steel-clad hoofs of Julietta were ringing on the pavement, sweeping her toward La Casa Vereal.

29

What should she do when she reached La Casa Vereal? Could she, without dying of shame at once, announce herself with her true name or allow the servants to see her face? She found that she could, and that it was a small thing to accomplish. With the butt of her quirt she beat at the locked gate, and when the servant's voice answered, she cried out: "It is Alicia Alvarado. Bring me quickly to your master. It is life or death—life or death!"

It was a name to conjure wide even a stronger gate than this. The wide, heavy panels swung back. She found herself looking down from the saddle into a frightened, staring face.

"Quickly! Quickly!"

She was out of the saddle at once and hurried at the flying heels of the porter. They entered the house. In the great hall she waited, where the darkness was only dimly broken by a single hanging lamp. Here was a chair, and yonder the great stairway began. But all the rest was thickest shadow. It seemed to her like a great tomb, already waiting for the death of a brave man.

She went to the casement that the fresh night air might come at her face, but from that window she was looking down over the pale stretch of San Triste, blanched in the moonshine. It seemed to Alicia that a dull roaring, as of many hoofs pounding up the slope to La Casa Vereal, had already begun; or was it only the thundering of her frightened heart? Would he never come?

He came at last, his clothes thrown hastily on; his eyes grave and yet eager; and she could see the shadow of a new sorrow upon his face. She did not waste time, but with a trembling voice she said to him: "Señor, the true Vereal has come. San Triste is being raised for him by many men—by my father and others. There are scores of ruffians at his back. Fly, señor, if you prize your life. Adieu!"

She was at the door before he reached her. There he stayed her, not with a touch, but merely with his raised hand. She shrank away a little. But her whole body was trembling with joy that there was still to be one moment with him; that the end had not yet come.

"You have fleet horses," she went on. "Take the very fastest. Ride, señor, ride!"

"You have heard the truth, then!" he said.

"All the truth—all the truth!"

"You know that I have lived a lie in San Triste?"

"I know it. But there is no time for such talk," she said, "when at any moment—"

"Hush," said he. "What is the anger of San Triste and what are its guns? They are nothing, I swear. There is nothing under heaven that is important except that I have you here for a last talk."

"But they are coming! Listen! I think I hear the beat of the horses on—"

He raised his head and looked out of the casement over the town, his eyes gleaming.

"Let them come," he said. "They shall not find me. My horse is saddled and ready, and it is such a horse as they will never be able to keep pace with for a single mile. They are nothing to me. If I could have had their love, Alicia, I swear to you that they would have thought the Vereal truly lived once more in this house. But as for their hate—I care nothing for it."

"Señor, I entreat you to go!"

"And leave you with only a half-knowledge of what I am? No, no! I want you to know the truth for the sake of the one thing in me, and that is my love for you."

She drew back a little, to support herself with one hand against the wall, but in the shadow he could not see that gesture, and saw only the shrinking from him.

"I have no more to expect," he said, growing white of face. "You scorn me, and you loathe me, Alicia, and God knows that I have given you cause. But I want you to know by what queer steps I've come to this. I can tell you all in a moment, and yet it is a strange story.

"I came out of college two years ago with consumption. They sent me West; and in a month or two I was sounder than oak. It was my country, do you see, although I had never been in it before. I had ridden all my life and handled guns all my life, but there is a difference between shooting at a target and shooting at a man; there is a difference between riding behind hounds and riding for one's life. I had been a hunter, but now I found out that the greatest thrill of all is to be the hunted.

"The hunter has his happiness in making a kill, but what is that compared with the thrill of the hunted thing which escapes? It came about in a queer way.

"I was leading a lonely life in a little shack in the mountains, cooking for myself, sleeping like a rock at night, and riding every day trying to cram something more of that God-given country into my memory before I left for the East. While I was out, a posse riding down a horse thief came on me.

"I rode a black horse and the thief had been riding one. That was all they knew, but they started after me, and I rode for my life. In an hour I was clear of them, but it was the most perfect hour of my life. I came off with a bullet through my hat and my horse Pierre in a lather, but I felt that I had had my first taste of true living.

"After that, I deliberately started to leave trails which could be followed for a distance and to give the officers of the law bait which would make them come after me. Does that sound like madness to you? I tell you, it was fascinating, and not so terribly dangerous, either. I mapped the country in my mind until I knew every trail and every turn in the district. I had a wonderful horse beneath me, and they never came near enough to tag me with a bullet.

"I put off the time of my return. Twice I went East to my family, resolved to settle down and become a hard-working man in my father's law office. Twice I failed to stay by my guns and had to come West again. Back I came to the old game.

"My true name is John Given. For my foolish life in the West I called myself John Jones. But they named me the Kid, because I was young. I had fights here and there; but I have never killed or even very seriously injured any man.

"I knew that I was playing with fire, but that was the beauty of the life. Of course, every crime that was committed by an unknown man was heaped on my shoulders. I was accused of everything from theft to murder. The sheriffs of half a dozen counties hunted me. But still I escaped.

"Then came these racals with their proposal that, because I looked like a Vereal, I should come down here and assume the name. It was only another chapter of foolish adventure to me, do you understand? There was another phase of it. Poor Joseph Simon had been kept out of a great fortune which belonged by justice to him. I wanted to see him get what was his own. So I came as they wished.

"But after I came here, two things happened. I felt, in my heart of hearts, that I could play the part of the Vereal for the city better than that heavy-minded brute, Cabrillo. But first and foremost, I saw you, Alicia, and from the instant I saw you, my life stopped and began again. There was only one great purpose before me, and that was to win your love.

"There was one wild moment," he said, "when I thought that you, too, cared for me. But I was wrong, Alicia, and even if I had been right, what you have learned about me would have made you despise me for a cheat! Is it so? In the name of God, Alicia, is it so?"

He could only see the whiteness of her face and of her hand, so buried was she in the shadow.

Then: "John," she whispered, "they are coming at last. Do you hear? Do you hear?"

Through the air came a deep, far-off humming of many voices, rolled together.

"You have not answered," he told her.

"Quickly, John! They are coming! They mean murder, and if you die—"

Her voice died, but in its frightened stopping he knew all that he could have wished to know.

He took her into the court and raised her into her saddle with strong arms. But: "I must not go—not until I have seen you mounted and away."

Back they went to the stables, and there, in the first stall, saddled and soon bridled, was Pierre. The black horse came dancing forth, eager for the night and whatever wild work lay before him. It seemed to her that he was like his master, terrible and swift, and strong. Surely they could not fail together.

He leaned above her, cherishing her close to him.

"But if you leave me," she whispered, "I must go back to my father. He will give me to Cabrillo, John. He has sworn to do that, and he is like a rock in determination. Tell me what to do."

He looked down over the white city of San Triste. It had never seemed more lovely to him than it was at that moment, and yet he knew in his heart of hearts that he must take her now or never.

"Alicia," he said, "will you ride with me?"

There was no exclamation, but only a little sigh of content.

"Dear John," she said, "I thought you would never ask me!"

30

The dawn came as Simon and his calvacade crossed the first range of mountains, and with the dawn they saw the blue of the ocean. It was still far, far away, but through a deep gap in the second range they could look down from the first and see that shimmering mass of blue. At that sight, Joseph Simon threw up his hands and cried: "The sea! The sea! Denny, we have won at last. Ulloa lies beyond that next range!"

"We ain't got over that range yet," said Silas Denny gravely.

He looked back over the line of thirty mules, strung out one by one, the head of the column already issuing through the pass and the rest still winding up the defile.

"We ain't over the last range yet," said Denny again, "and when we *do* get over, we got soft sand for the going all the way to the pier. Besides, these mules are beat."

"They're not sweating very greatly," said Joseph Simon, cocking his head upon one side and looking earnestly at the mules. "They're not sweating as much as my horse, for instance."

Denny cast a glance of disgust at him, as though such ignorance was almost too blind to deserve enlightenment. But he said at the last: "A horse sweats outside and a mule sweats inside. Those mules are spent, I say. Look at their ears and their eyes."

For the eyes were dull and the long ears flopped up and down, but never rolled forward.

"Not much hell in those eyes," said Silas Denny, "and when a mule stops having the devil in him, it means that he's about all in."

There was a sharp voice in Spanish from the rear of the mule train. Some one had sighted horsemen following fast on their heels.

"God forbid!" cried Joseph Simon, turning white as a ghost. "God forbid that just as the cup is at our lips it should be dashed away. But a curse is on me and mine in Mexico!"

He began to wring his hands, but Silas Denny turned without a word and went back to the rear of the mule train. He could see at once the cause of the disturbance. Four mounted figures had broken out from among the trees and headed up toward them in the pass. Si Denny looked hastily about him. Joseph Simon was useless with weapons, and most of the muleteers were not at home with guns.

But Denny, during the long night march, had chosen two of the men who were quite capable of giving a good account of themselves even in the face of a most formidable peril. He had so far taken them into his confidence that he had assured them the march through the night might be interrupted, and he had asked them if they were willing to fight for their own lives and the lives of their employers. He had gone even further, telling them frankly what they had already guessed.

"These mules are loaded with gold, amigos," he had said to them. "Can you imagine what your reward will be if you fight to save it for us?"

Their grins had spread broad upon their swarthy faces. They would fight, he knew, until the last blood was out of their bodies, partly for the sake of the money there might be in it, partly for the sake of the preference which had been given in picking them out above their comrades, and perhaps above all else because they loved battle for its own sake. He had given them the rifles at that time, and all through the march they had been constantly fingering the weapons. They were ready to use them now. With their backing he thought nothing of any attack which might be delivered by four men, no matter who they might be.

He bade the train of mules move on. With his two assistants, he crouched in the throat of the pass, unlimbered his own rifle, and couched it lovingly in the hollow of his shoulder. His companions did the same without a word, but with a most meaning swiftness and deft ease in their handling of the guns. So he came to draw his bead, while the four were still well out of effective range, but he had barely centered the first figure when one of the peons cried out: "A woman!" Dropping his rifle, he pointed.

There could be no doubt about it. Si Denny, rubbing his eyes and then straining them toward the approaching quartet, saw them move out of the shadow of a hollow and into the sun on the top of a swell of the ground. Then he could distinguish her clearly enough, riding in the rear couple of the four with the sun glittering on her sweating horse. Not only that, but he thought his straining eyes recognized the shapely figure of the animal which her companion bestrode, and the next instant his premonition was given a body by a second shout from the same sharp-eyed peon.

"El Vereal!"

Si Denny cursed softly to himself. "I knew it! Marmont was right!" he muttered to himself. "A woman was at the bottom of all the trouble—the devil fly away from them all! there's the Kid—and Halsey and Marmont with him, by heaven!"

For it was indeed they. They came rapidly into close range, now, until their faces could be distinguished. Their horses were staggering, but still they drove the weary nags on relentlessly, leaning in their saddles to jockey a trifling bit greater speed out of the poor brutes and still glancing now and again, involuntarily, back over their shoulders. They were

pursued, and desperately close. There could be no doubt of
that, though still the enemy was out of sight among the hills.

They drove in still closer, and now the peon and Denny
spoke with one voice: "The Señorita Alvarado!"

"Damn my eyes," said Denny to himself. "The Kid picks
only the best while he's about it. Alicia Alvarado! All of San
Triste will go mad when this is known!"

But here was the little squadron of four upon them: Halsey
with his face drawn and wrinkled with pain, and his arm in
the sling; Marmont with a black frown on his brow and his
jaw thrust out in murderous determination; and Alicia and the
Kid, alias John Jones, alias John Given, as radiant and as gay
as though they had barely started on a pleasure jaunt in the
cool of the morning. Who could have guessed, from their
flushed and happy faces, that they had been riding since
midnight?

"This is what met us," said Marmont gloomily. "This!"

He turned upon Alicia a glance of such glowering disapproval that Denny wrinkled his long nose and shook his head.
For his own part, though there was little enough similarity
between their faces, he was looking back to a certain maiden
in a New England village, many a hard year ago, who had
taken a farewell walk with him as he started out to make his
fortune in the wide world.

What fortunes they had been, to be sure! He had never
seen her again, but still her face was as bright in his memory
as though it was yesterday that he had said good-by.

So Denny took off his hat and stood beside Alicia Alvarado.

"Señorita," he said, "I am happy to see you; but I'm
mighty sorry to see you here!"

She laughed down at him. "We have been playing a game
half the night," she said. "As John puts it, they have tagged
me only once!"

She raised the skirt of her jacket; it was punctured with a
neat little round hole of just the size of a .38 caliber bullet
would make. Si Denny turned a sick face to the Kid, and the
Kid looked sickly back to him.

"I know," the Kid said humbly.

"You know!" sneered Denny. "By heaven, for taking her into a thing like this—"

"Enough!" broke in Marmont. "She is here. *That* cannot be changed. Now, Denny, tell me. The stuff is on the ship now and you, like a brave comrade, have waited here to keep a lookout for us?"

"The mules are in the hollow," said Denny, "making for the next range. We've still got some long minutes before us before they'll get to the pier, and when we get them to the pier, there's still the unloading to be done. There's plenty to unload, too."

Marmont threw up his hands with a shout of rage.

"Blockhead!" he cried. "Fool!"

"Mules have no wings," said Denny sullenly. "We pushed them ahead as fast as we could."

Marmont had fallen into dumb despair. He made a gesture. He could not speak all that was in his mind.

"They're hot behind us," interrupted Halsey, looking back with a sigh. "We outdared them and outrode them and besides, we were better mounted, and that's the only reason we're this breathing space ahead of them."

"Who are 'them'?" asked Denny.

"Half of San Triste. I don't know how many, but you can put a wager that only the best mounted are coming behind us after the pace we've set for them. In a word, Denny, young Vereal and Cabrillo got away from us."

"Ten thousand devils!"

"A million devils, if you choose. How they managed it, we don't know. They were alone half a minute while I tried to persuade Marmont not to cut their throats and so make our work a trifle easier. Before I was through persuading, the two of them were loose. We barely got off with our lives, because with one arm, I was in no shape to stand up and take my share in a hand-to-hand fight.

"We bolted for Ulloa. In the meantime, they came as fast as though they were on a train. They reached San Triste, convinced Alvarado that they had the real Vereal, raised the town with his help, and would have trapped the Kid if the señorita had not brought him warning.

"He rode, and she came with him with those yelling devils at their heels. The two of them came up with us—we hadn't been pushing our horses as fast as we might on account of the pain in my arm. That tells the story. Except for one thing—by the yells we heard behind us, during the last hour or so, we know that Grenacho and his pack of half-starved wolves is leading the procession. That means trouble, my friend Denny!"

Denny's face had showed various emotions as he listened to this brief recital of calamities; but when it was ended he merely shrugged his shoulders.

'They'll have the mules and their packs before we can get them up the slope to the farther side," he said quietly. "Perhaps they'll have us, too. At least, old Simon will die of a broken heart if he's robbed again. Look!" he muttered.

For the Kid and Alicia de Alvarado had drawn apart, not to speak, but merely to gaze on each other with unutterable joy.

"It was that way all night," snarled out Marmont. "They sang songs while Grenacho's fiends showered bullets around their heads. They're both insane."

"We'll see about that," said Halsey. He added more loudly: "Hello, Jones!"

The Kid turned his smiling face toward them.

"How do we stop that mob of devils and give ourselves a chance to get to the ship?" asked Halsey.

The Kid looked more soberly around him. Then he turned to the girl. "Alicia," he said, "ride on straight across the pass and follow the trail. You'll find the mule train in the hollow beneath. Stay with them. In a moment we'll come."

"And you?" she murmured, lingering.

"Trust my luck today," he answered, and so, waving to him, she cantered her tired horse through the pass and out of sight.

"There is only one way," said the Kid without the slightest emotion, joining the three. "We must do what they do when the wolves come too close to the sleigh. Throw one of the passengers overboard and keep them busy for a minute or two!"

31

For all his gaiety it was plain that he meant what he said, and Marmont asked him to be clearer. It was simple when he had spoken half a dozen words. The pass was wide enough at the top, when the mountaintops rolled back on either side, but its throat was narrow. There was barely a trail for a single horse.

One man, well armed and determined, could make his position in the neck of the pass good for an indefinite time, even against such desperate and wily fighters as Grenacho's men. It was with these that they would undoubtedly have to contend.

Riding as often by night as by day, inured to every fatigue of the saddle, mounted upon half-wild mustangs of no great speed of foot but tireless in energy, and able to gallop all day without halting, Grenacho and his savage followers would doubtless have far distanced the men of San Triste, no matter how gallantly the latter strove to keep up with the pace. The rush of the outlaws, unhampered by the timidity or irresolution or the ignorance of the others in the pursuit, would be a terrible danger to face.

There was no hesitation among the four. The chances of each were four to one against losing, and they blithely threw their coins. Halsey and Denny were eliminated in the first matching; in the second, the Kid called the coin of Marmont, and the Frenchman, stooping slowly and raising the bit of silver, straightened by gradual degrees. For he would not let them see his face while the first horror was upon it. When he was erect again, he was smiling.

One by one, the others said good-by to him, gravely and yet not with any false pity. For, had the chance fallen to one of the others, they all knew that Marmont would have been whistling contentedly ten seconds after he had turned his back on his doomed comrade. The Frenchman, however, carried the matter off with the best of spirits.

"They will never put their bullets in me," he said confidently. "I'll hold them off until dark. Then I'll slip away and get to Ulloa. Or perhaps you can send help back to me from the town. Adieu! Adieu!"

They left him, silent, full of their thoughts, and as they wound out of sight down the hollow of the pass, they heard him singing the stirring refrain of the Marseillaise. It was a last touch of bravado which Marmont could not resist. The other three looked at one another with faint smiles which were not smiles of mirth. Even Denny was touched.

"A brave fellow!" Halsey said. "A devil, a heartless rogue, but a brave fellow. God rest him!"

They pushed on for the caravan.

In the meantime, the Frenchman couched himself on the outer lip of the pass, where he could lie at the opening between two great black rocks and command the full slope beneath him. He had hardly taken up his position when the enemy were in sight. They came into view over the rolling hills like foam over a high-breaking sea. What they had expected was the case, for the men of San Triste, valiantly as they had striven, even Señor Alvarado on his best horse and with the anxiety of a father to spur him on, had not been able to keep pace with these savage warriors.

Their mustangs were at a steady lope, many of them staggering at their work, but still the whole body advanced with astonishing regularity and speed so closely bunched as to be in hand for a surprise attack at any time.

These things Marmont noted. He had been a soldier in his day, and he knew as he scanned their bearing that his last hour had come. These men would fight like wild beasts until they conquered or died. They were Indians, most of them. A few were renegade Americans, more savage than any barbarians. Altogether, there were thirty-odd horsemen. There were enough, at least, to assure Marmont that he had come to the end of his rope, with no hope of escape.

Therefore, methodically he prepared himself for his death. He was surprised at his own procedure. He had been in many a terrible danger before, but in none that was hopeless on the face of it, and in none against which he had so much time to prepare. He found himself doing things which he had forgotten since his childhood. He kneeled, crossed himself, and with closed eyes, his face raised until the light of the sun made the blood in his eyelids a red smear across his vision he strove to recollect all his sins.

What black swarms they were! They flooded across his mind in droves. There had not been a year of his life that had not seen its wrongdoing, from the childish times when he had pilfered from his school comrades, from his brothers, from his parents. He had passed on to greater sins. The smaller things dropped out of his vision. He saw the red marks of the killings which he had committed with his own hands. There was one man slain in his sleep. Marmont shuddered with horror as he thought of that.

"But God," said Marmont, groaning out the words, "is all-merciful! Holy Virgin, intercede for my wretched name!"

He crossed himself again, and rose.

It was none too soon, for the troop had crossed a great distance in the meantime. He could begin to mark even their faces. Still they swept nearer and nearer. He drew his first bead. It was a squat, broad-shouldered figure who rode in the very midst of the front rank, the others sloping off on either side of him, his features shaded by the great, stiff brim of an expensive sombrero, though the rest of his costume was as shabby as that of the others. Instinctively, Marmont knew that this was Grenacho. If, with a lucky first bullet, he could kill this man, he felt that the others might be seized with a panic.

Grenacho, then, was the central form in his mind's eye, but he selected, also, two others on either side of the leader. For he determined, after the first shot, to deliver several others in close succession, to give the impression, as nearly as he was able, of a number of men, firing almost in a volley.

The speed of the repeating Winchester would help him in
this.

He centered the sights, drew a careful aim, and then
squeezed the trigger. The gun spoke loud, and he saw
Grenacho flinch to one side of his saddle, but still the squat
figure did not fall from the saddle.

"A clear miss. The devil is against me today," thought
Marmont, and while he thought, as fast as he could pull the
trigger, he pumped four more shots into the advancing troop.
One man fell; another twisted halfway around in his saddle
with a yell; the others scattered on either side to find shelter,
while their shouts washed in a deafening roar to Marmont in
his hiding place. Almost before he could put in another
bullet, they were ensconced behind rocks, a number of which
littered the hillside.

His nerves grew quieter after this. He told himself that at
the next trial he would make a better score by far than that of
one bull's-eye out of four attempts. In the meantime he drew
back behind the rock and replenished his magazine.

How far had the train of mules gone toward safety, now?
He saw the faces of his companions one by one, and presently
he said aloud, simply: "They are all better men than I. Even
Simon is a better man."

Marmont looked forth again, in time to try a snapshot at
two figures which were rushing up the slope to gain a more
advanced rock. Their yells of triumph told him that he had
missed; at the same time, half a dozen bullets spattered with
heavy shocks on the face of the rocks behind which he was
sheltered, and one hummed wickedly through the gap between them.

This was not Indian shooting; these fellows were prize
marksmen, all of them. The greatest miracle was that they
had been able to fire their shots, and so many of them,
without showing to him as much as an arm or a hand. He had
only seen the twinkle of the sunlight on rifle barrels, here and
there.

He bit his lip, and then shifted his position a few yards to
the right. A hat showed above a rock. He drilled it with a fine
center shot and was instantly greeted with a mocking shout

while the hat itself was pushed higher upon the twig which supported it. He had wasted a bullet. This was a small matter, but he had also betrayed his new position for nothing, and he soon had cause to regret it.

For the stones before him were much smaller than those which had been his recent shelter, and now the air about him was constantly searched by whining bullets, and he could not move back to his former place without the greatest risk. He wished that he had not moved.

However, they could now advance no farther, for there were no rocks to shelter them. He could afford to lie flat on his face, looking out only from time to time to make sure that they were not launching any concerted rush against his position.

The minutes rolled on, and with the passage of every second he carried a picture in his mind's eye of the caravan trooping slowly ahead, the riders keeping an anxious lookout behind them. He saw, sadly and wonderingly, that this thing was all that he had ever done in the course of his life to help a fellow mortal. Even this service might be of no avail.

The thought had barely entered his mind when a blow was struck on the sand beside him and a shower of stinging sand spray was dashed against his cheek. The sing of the bullet followed and then the heavy, clanging report of the rifle. He looked up, for the sound had come from the side of the pass far above him. At the same time, a shout of triumph roared up from the men of Grenacho who were gathered beneath, waiting.

He understood then, and anger rushed through his brain. They had tricked him, and simply enough. While he stared down from his covert and watched the rocks before him, one or two of the party had circled to the left and climbed to the height. From that safe position they could shoot him down at their leisure and with perfect safety.

While he looked up, he saw the wink of the sun on a rifle barrel. He snatched up his own weapon and fired. There was an instant's pause, and then a heavy blow was struck him which knocked him back on his face. A rifle ball had crunched through his left shoulder.

It half dazed him. When he had a clear brain again, he saw that his cause was lost indeed. The weirdly pitched yell of the warrior above him was informing Grenacho's men that their enemy had been struck down. They could not wait for a surety, but now he heard the rush of their feet. He caught at his rifle; it was an unwieldy bulk in his hand. He could not fire another shot with it. But to die here helplessly was more than he could endure. He would die fighting even though he could not shoot.

He caught his rifle halfway down the barrel with his sinewy right hand. Then, swinging the weapon as a club, he charged out from behind his rock and faced the sweep of thirty yelling madmen.

It seemed to Marmont that those directly before him flinched back a little when they saw his wild attack coming. But one burly fellow rushed at him, firing a revolver rapidly. Marmont felt a bullet sear his cheek. Another plucked at his nerveless, ruined left arm. Then he brained the fellow with a sweeping blow of the butt. The next instant a knife was in his throat and a bullet through his head. He died without a word.

32

Those who hurried the staggering mules through the gap in the second range could tell the second of the fall of Marmont by the wild yell of triumph which arose from the men of Grenacho. They heard it at the very moment when they could look down to their goal of safety. At the foot of the long slope which rippled to the sea was the little village and port of Ulloa.

It was a port by rare courtesy. A single pier, decorated with a few shacks by way of storehouses, stretched a shambling length into the blue waters of the Gulf, and beside the pier lay a long-bodied, rakish little ship from whose stack the smoke was streaming. Macpherson had been as good as his word, and his ship was ready to leap out to sea.

How welcome was that sight to the hounded travelers. The very mules seemed to know that the end of the journey was near at hand. Joseph Simon, in a frenzy of joy and anxiety, was offering new hundreds to the tired muleteers if they would but club the staggering beasts into Ulloa in time.

They did not need money to urge them forward now. They had heard the scream of Grenacho's wolf pack in the distance, and each man promised himself no better than a dog's death unless the caravan reached Ulloa and safety in time. They sprang to their work with yells and in a fury of haste. With one hand they belabored the pack animals. With the other they jerked them forward by the head. So the whole line broke into a stumbling, fumbling trot and swept down toward Ulloa and the sea and the *Rachel* lying beside the pier.

It was at the same instant that the shouting of the pursuers drew nearer, then dipped suddenly into dimness and apparently greater distance. By that, they could know that Grenacho had left the higher pass and was sweeping ahead with frantic speed down that first slope, knowing well how near his booty was to escape.

But Ulloa itself would be no shelter for the fugitives. Its handful of inhabitants would not risk their lives for the sake of a handful of gringos.

They would take to their heels and lie in cover until the fighting was over and Grenacho's enemies were dead. Then they would come forth idly, to look at the scene of the strife. No, Ulloa was not a refuge. But at the end of the rickety pier—that was the place for them.

There were men moving on that pier. Doubtless they were the crew of Macpherson, and if they would not fight in an unknown cause, at least they would be sure to give a hand with the loading of that precious cargo. That was the goal, and with the horror rushing upon them from the rear, it seemed sadly distant indeed.

The last of the happiness was gone from the face of Alicia.

She rode with her eyes fixed wistfully upon John Given. He wasted not a moment when the sound of Grenacho's rush was heard behind them, but he said to her: "Alicia, bullets may be stirring here before long. You must ride on ahead—ride to the *Rachel*—tell the captain that we are coming. Urge him in God's name if he has a care either to save the lives of hard-pressed men or to line his own pockets with gold to send us aid.

"If he will go no farther, at least line up his crew at the foot of the pier in one of the shacks. That will give us a nearer goal. We can stand off their rush there, while the mules are unloaded. Quickly, Alicia!"

She was off in a twinkling, riding desperately. The peons and Simon were already a little distance ahead with the struggling mules. The three drew close together.

"It is the same game once more," said the Kid. "The odd man stays in the second pass, friends! Are you ready?"

They were ready without a word. They held their coins balanced upon their thumbs. They tossed them winking and spinning into the air. They spattered down again into the sand, a head for the Kid, a head for Si Denny, a tail for poor Halsey.

"It can't be this way," said the Kid hastily. "I forgot, Halsey. A man with one arm—"

"Is as good as two, lad," said the Englishman mildly. "Just as good as two in such a game as this. Noise is all that anybody can make to keep back those devils. I'll tell you a secret—an Englishman with only one hand can make as much noise as a Frenchman with two. Ride on, lad. Ride on, Denny."

He shook hands with them. Into the hand of the Kid he pressed a thin wallet.

"You'll find a picture in it and an address," said Halsey. "Send the picture. Tell them—that I was an honest man, of course. About to hit it lucky in a mine. You understand. Something to cheer them up. You knew me for years. If you go to the other side, one of these days, drop in at the place. It's a lovely little corner of old Devon. Good-by, my friend!"

He turned his horse up the hill, while Denny and the Kid

looked sadly after him. One fearless man had gone before and paid for all his sins in a fine death. Now another of the fearless was to be sacrificed.

"For what?" cried Si Denny in a sudden outbreak of fury. "For Simon's gold; may it all be damned! Kid, let's call him back."

"Do you think he would come?" asked the Kid.

Silas Denny sighed.

"Look at him now," he said. "A queer fellow was Halsey."

He put the brave Englishman naturally enough in the past tense, for there was no hope. The first pass had been twice as defensible. This second one was a wide-mouthed opening through which twenty men could ride abreast. Toward the sea side of it, the Englishman was slowly walking his horse, for there was time enough for him to get into his position.

As he rode, they saw him take a small whisk broom out of his saddlebag. With it, he went carefully over his clothes. He dropped it back in the bag. They saw him remove his hat and smooth down his hair. No doubt he was doing these things automatically, while his mind was on other things, but nevertheless, even automatically, he was making himself presentable for his death.

"A darned queer fellow," repeated Si Denny. "I dunno but that I sort of like his fool ways, though."

The Kid, smiling faintly at his companion, made no reply, but he jogged on with Denny after the mules. Reeling and sweating and groaning, the poor pack train was struggling on toward Ulloa and peace, but every step was a step of misery. They were still half a mile away when the rear-most mule sank suddenly to the earth and lay there.

It was dead when they came to it. So the gold was taken from the pack and distributed in the saddle pockets of the men. Joseph Simon, hoarse of voice, rode up and down the line, begging, cursing, imploring the muleteers to greater efforts.

Had all his promises been remembered on this day, they would have beggared a new Croesus in their fulfillment. But what he said the muleteers did not understand, saving only the two armed peons who walked in the rear of the train, sullenly ready to pay for their keep with bullets when the time for action came. They were the last hope—the rear guard—and knowing it well, they handled their rifles and prepared for action.

As for their fellows who were beating the leg-weary mules along the trail, they were hysterical with terror, now. At any moment they were apt to bolt for Ulloa or a nearer shelter if one offered to them, for their pace afoot would far outstrip the speed of the pack train.

So they crawled toward Ulloa, bit by bit, the distance seemed all at once to lengthen to weary miles when the crash of rifles came ringing from the pass. They were at poor Halsey. Could he keep them back for even a second? Or would they wash across his body in a single wave?

The muleteers, grimacing with fear, wavered and prepared to bolt, but the roar of the guns did not cease. The lively babel continued in the hollow heart of the pass; Halsey was keeping his word.

They reached the outskirts of Ulloa, and the muleteers, as their animals swung onto the better going of the one long, winding street, uttered a frantic yell of triumph. The hope of ultimate success was taking the place of terror. Even the mules, conscious that a town meant a halting place after such a terrible march, went forward with a faintly renewed vigor. Still, from the pass far behind them, the rifles were ringing, ringing—then suddenly ceased, and a wild yell broke through the air and came swinging down to their ears who listened in that street in Ulloa.

Halsey was dead!

The manner of his death they never were to know, only having in their minds the miracle of the thing which he had done. For he had kept thirty fighting men employed for priceless minutes while the train wound its heavy way toward safety. Now that they were at the very door of success, he had succumbed to the pressure.

"There is one thing sure," said Si Denny. "That is that it took more than one bullet to kill Halsey, God bless him. There was no fear in that man!"

Halsey was dead indeed. Two bullets had passed through

his brain—his arms were stretched out crosswise on the sands—his face was turned calmly to the sky.

His last words were these: "What bully good regulars those rascals would make if they'd stand discipline!"

The last of the pack train was halfway down the street of Ulloa when a shrill cry from the peons announced that the enemy was in sight again. All looked back, and they saw the horsemen of Grenacho streaming down from the pass. They could be easily counted, and Denny numbered them at twenty-five. Certainly Halsey had made them pay for his death.

Still the muleteers flogged the mules ahead. They rattled down the street with Joseph Simon screaming to every man who showed his head at a door a frantic appeal for help—a fabulous offer of reward. But not a man stirred to aid him. The word had come before them; Grenacho was at their heels, and what Grenacho marked down for his prey would be wise for other men to leave alone. So they came to the foot of the pier and the sight of the crew of the *Rachel.*

33

There were seven hardy rascals, seven of the scum of the seas headed by a short, fat, red-faced Scotchman. That was Macpherson with his crew. He had hand-picked them from odd corners and quarters of the globe. There was a Malay, a Portuguese, a Finn, a Gold Coast Negro of gigantic size, a wide-mouthed Dane, and a little withered, black-eyed Neapolitan.

One could have searched the world over again without finding such another collection of villains. Macpherson had his own reasons for his choices. One reason was that he could have any man of that crew hung in any port of the world for heinous offenses against humanity. He liked to have men like that under him. For one thing, it made them amenable to discipline. For who minds a blow from one who may hang you when he chooses?

These renegades greeted the approaching caravan with a cheer as the tired mules stepped onto the pier.

"Mr. Macpherson? Mr. Macpherson?" shouted Joseph Simon. "Where is Mr. Macpherson?"

"Stop blathering about a mister," said the sailor. "I'm Captain Macpherson, if that's what you mean."

"Captain, in the name of God give us help to get these packs aboard your ship."

"I'll do my part," said Macpherson.

He eyed the packs shrewdly—their smallness and their apparent weight.

"Because," cried Simon, "the robbers are at our heels. See them coming. They ride like devils—and devils they are. They would murder us all!"

"Think they would that," said the captain, cocking his round hat upon one side. "I think that they would that. Unless we murdered them first. But I didn't bargain for a battle as well as a cruise. My rate goes up."

"To what?"

"It's doubled, my friend."

"Granted—granted—and five thousand more besides to see us safely aboard and all out to sea."

Macpherson saw that if his greed had not made him hasty he might have pitched his robbery in a higher scale. He might have demanded and received five—ten times as much as he had at first asked.

However, when a bargain was once made, he was a man of his word; that is to say, he was a man of his word within certain limits. While the peons rushed the mules up the pier, and while the men of Grenacho were already sweeping through the town of Ulloa, Captain Macpherson ordered his crew to turn heartily and tumble the cargo aboard.

"Drop nothing overboard, you swine!" bellowed Macpherson. "For darn me if there's not the price of ten crews like you in every one of those little bags."

Here he was seized by a slender hand, strong as flexible iron. He turned and confronted the Kid.

"If you put to sea without me," said the Kid quietly, "take that lady to New York and bring her to John Given, Senior. You will find his name in the directory."

"I'm to do that for the sake of her face, eh?" inquired Macpherson sneeringly.

"My father will pay you twice the price you ask for the sake of the news which you'll bring him about his son."

The sailor gasped.

"Now take her aboard," said the Kid. "Lock her in a cabin from which she can see nothing that goes on on the pier. Do you understand?"

The captain blinked, nodded, and then, turning, he deftly passed his arm through the arm of Alicia. She shrank from him, crying: "John, are you leaving me?"

But John Given, Jr., was running down the pier, drawing his revolver as he went. A gust of the freshening sea breeze which was tossing the waves into sharp crests out in the bay knocked the hat from his head. His hair blew wild upon his head, and so he ran into the battle.

He arrived in the nick of time. Grenacho's bull voice was shouting orders. His men, gathering to a solid head, having dismounted from their horses, swept straight up the pier at the first shack. In that shack, as the Kid arrived, he found Si Denny, as big and as cool as ever, his rifle at his shoulder while he drew a methodical bead.

Beside the big American were the two peons, shaking with fear, but with their minds made up to play the part of men on this day. They had rifles also, but the Kid was content with his revolver. It was a faster gun; there was another in the holster at his left hip to replace it when the first was emptied, and at such close quarters his aim would be as excellent as though a rifle was in his hands.

So equipped, they met that first charge and blasted the head of the column out of existence. Even Grenacho's men wavered in front of such a fire. They scrambled for shelter behind boxes and piles of coiled ropes and steel cable. From these shelters they poured in their return volleys, riddling the storehouse from side to side with every shot.

At the very first discharge one of the peons dropped on his face with a gurgling cry and lay still, and the cheek of Si Denny was laid open. A moment later the second peon dropped, and the Kid was pale from a shallow wound on his left arm.

But still his revolvers and the rifle of Denny made deadly play until, looking back through the rear window of the shack, they could see that the last of the packs were being stripped from the mules and tossed over the rail of the little *Rachel*.

More, they could see the cable of the *Rachel* thrown clear of the mooring bar, and then the little ship herself swung her head away from the pier, tossed out by the waves.

"By the eternal," shouted Si Denny. "The dogs are leaving us here to be murdered, while we fight for the gold. Kid, if you're fast on your feet, try to beat me down the pier!"

He was through the door in a twinkling. Fast as he raced, however, he was no match for the fleet-footed Kid. The latter drifted up to him and passed him, but already the Mexicans, the moment the gunfire from the shack stopped, had rushed into it and around it and now they were storming down the pier yelling like demons.

The Kid, in the meantime, reached the side of the *Rachel* and sprang aboard with a whistle of bullets past his ears to give him lighter wings in his leap. But still the *Rachel* hung in her place.

The propeller of the little ship was churning the water, but heavy waves were washing dead against her bows, driving her back. She stirred and drifted forward, but still she was hugging the side of the wharf, and it would be a simple thing for the rush of Grenacho's human tigers to master her.

On they came like a flood, waving their guns, seeing victory in their grasp at last, after so long and bitter a struggle for it. Grenacho himself ran in the front with an amazing agility for a man past his youth. He even gained upon long-striding Si Denny.

So much the Kid saw in his first backward glance as he reached the deck of the *Rachel*. What he next saw was Denny pitching to his face on the pier. A random shot had struck him down.

He was not killed, however. The Kid saw him leap again to his feet and, with a single glance, measure his chances. He was close indeed to the *Rachel*, which was still grinding away along the side of the long pier, slowly gathering speed, but he was still more fatally close to the leading outlaws. He seemed to make up his mind in that split part of a second that he had found something worth dying for.

It seemed to the Kid, watching with a horrible fascination, daring not fire lest his bullet should strike down Denny himself, that the big Yankee, as he swung about, waved an arm in farewell. Then he witnessed a strange thing indeed, for Denny, with arms flung wide, met the sweep of the many men and checked them like a grown man stopping the rush of boys.

The Kid could stand no more. "Keep heart, Denny!" he shouted. "I'm coming!"

He rushed for the rail. He did not reach it. A stunning blow caught him on the side of the head and floored him. He looked up through a haze, and saw the burly, tubby form of Macpherson standing above him.

"There's enough bloodshed out yonder," he said. "No need for a young fool to throw himself away. Fighting is fighting, and by the eternal I like it, but murder is murder, and by the eternal, I hate it! You'll stay here, my fine spark!"

The Kid, groaning, reached his knees. He saw Si Denny, the central figure in a wildly twisting tangle of humanity. The bandits swarmed at him and over him, but they could not go past. His great rawboned fists were plying like sledgehammers, and every time they struck, a man fell.

There was the flash of knives and the sway of bone-crushing gun butts to beat him down, but still he stood, miraculously fighting on. Twice he staggered under that weight of humanity. Once he dropped to his knees, and the Kid thought that the horrible end had come. But still the heart of Si Denny was the heart of a giant.

He rose once more to his feet. He had caught a man by the feet and now he swung that body around his head as an athlete swings a hammer. One sweeping circle—then he flung his victim in the face of the enemy. It gained him an instant's advantage. He drove straight ahead, disdaining to retreat. Perhaps he had already felt his death wound in the struggle.

John Given, maddened at the sight, struggled again to get to the rail. It was too late. The *Rachel,* coming clear of the pier, was answering her helm at last and sheering rapidly away from danger. Ten feet of open water separated her from the edges of the piles already, and she was fast increasing that precious distance.

All that the Kid could do was to stand and gaze and wonder, for still Denny refused to die, and still the knot of struggling men twisted and writhed about him. At length he was down. The gleam of a knife blade was extinguished in his body; and that was the death of the last of the fearless.

There were no prayers on the lips of the big Yankee as he died, but the Kid, who had seen it all, wondered in his heart of hearts if this had not been the finest death of all the three.

He turned away, heartsick, dizzy. The Mexicans were raving on the pier as they saw their prize drift out to sea; the air was filled with the whining of their bullets; but the little *Rachel,* gathering head rapidly, was proving herself a greyhound of the ocean. She trembled with the drive of her engines. The whirling propeller lifted her forward and forward with lurches, like a horse rushing from the starting post and swinging into its stride.

But the Kid paid no heed either to the work of the *Rachel* or to the bullets of Grenacho's men. He was staring in astonishment at a strange picture on the deck of the little ship. It was Joseph Simon, kneeling among the bags of his treasure which was truly his at the last, with the tears streaming down his face and his happy eyes raised to the heavens.

"It is the will of God," said Joseph Simon.

The Kid, listening, thought of the three men who had died for this.

34

The joys of Joseph Simon were not ended, however. Neither were the strangenesses of the Kid. When they reached New Orleans, the Kid resolutely refused to touch a cent of the share of the plunder which was his due—by far the greatest share, as compared with the other three—for all that they had managed to do was to act as the merest accessories of the scheme which his own daring and cleverness had made possible. For himself, however, he would not take a penny, but he insisted that each of the three dead men should receive the portion that had been due him and that it should be rendered to their heirs.

So the money was left in trust, and by no means grudgingly on the part of Joseph Simon, for, as he was always fond of saying, it was the will of heaven which had restored to him the thing which was his and which had been taken away from him by misfortune and the injustice of man. Since it was the will of heaven which had restored to him that which was his, those who had assisted him were the direct agents of the Lord.

"For consider, Mr. Given," he would say, after he had learned the real name of the Kid, "that everything connected with our work had something miraculous about it. First there was that inspired thought about the portrait which came to me. Thereafter came that rare chance of finding the man who looked so like the picture that it might almost have been taken as a portrait of him.

"Consider still further that for my scheme I needed assistants—helpers who would be men both of courage and of cunning. In all of this I was successful and gathered together almost without effort three fearless men. Not one among them failed me, but all fought as though my cause was their own.

"Consider, finally, this thing, my young friend: through our endeavors, the true Vereal was recalled and brought into his property and his true mame, which would never have been if it had not been for our adventure. No, no, Mr. Given, the hand of God was in this matter, and for my part, not a cent of the treasure shall I ever use. It is consecrated gold."

"But," cried Given, amazed almost beyond speech, "do you mean this?"

"I do. I shall make it a gift to some good cause. There are great schools in our country which need support—schools which work for Frenchman and Englishman and American. To one of these I shall give the money."

"Why, Mr. Simon," said the Kid, "this is a noble thing to do. I wish you a long life of happiness for such a thought, but consider that the money is really all yours and that you and your father worked for it and made it honestly."

Joseph Simon cleared his throat and colored a little. "After all," he said, "I shall not greatly miss it. In the story which I first told you under the shadow of the Diablo Mountains, all was true. But one thing I a trifle understated. I told you that when I came back from Mexico I went into business and had some good fortune. Well, my friend, my fortune was more than good. Whatever I touched turned to gold. My thousands grew, in short, to millions. It was only the thought that the money hidden in La Casa Vereal was, after all, really mine and wrongfully kept from me, that spurred me to take such great risks."

"It cost the lives of three brave men," said the Kid solemnly.

"It gave three rascals an opportunity to redeem themselves for all their sins by gallant deaths in which they sacrificed themselves for the welfare of others," said Simon calmly. "I sorrow for them, but I cannot regret one thing which has been the outcome of this expedition."

As for the Kid, he did not choose to argue against this

point of view, for he was more than half convinced that Joseph Simon was right. Moreover, he had affairs of his own which occupied his mind very strictly.

They consisted in the jovial celebration of his return to his home, amd of the preparations for a wedding, and of Alicia in snowy white and in creamy lace, and of the opening of a home, and of the beginning of a business career.

But sometimes, in the brisk autumn of the year, when the hounds had made the kill and the hunt hacked slowly homeward through lanes embowered in crimson and gold, the head of John Given lifted and his glance went far away into a distant kingdom of thought which was filled with mighty, naked mountains and hot deserts. Or it went south to the white city of San Triste, dreaming under the sun.

It was not the last he saw of the men he had known in San Triste. On a day a card was brought to him inscribed with the name of Emile Fleuriot. He himself hurried out to the hall and met the tall old man with the stern face. He would have shaken his hand, but Emile prevented it with the lowest of bows.

"Señor Don José Vereal," said the valet, "presents his compliments, and wishes to know if his card would be unwelcome at the house of Mr. John Given."

"Tell Señor Vereal," said John Given, "that I am waiting most eagerly to see him."

He came the very next day, a gaier and more handsome young fellow than ever, and he sat on the edge of his chair to tell John Given of all that had happened in San Triste, and how the failure of Grenacho in that wild pursuit across the mountains had cost him the confidence of his band—of how they had murdered their famous leader and become themselves dissolved—of how San Triste still slept beneath the sun—of how the income of the estate gradually declined—of how its tenants daily prospered. So spoke young Don José, and shrugged his shoulders and laughed as he spoke.

"But after all," he said, "one cannot take money from the earth and carry it to heaven. Let them have what will make them happy. Enough remains for me. Enough, I hope, will remain for my children after me."

"Tell me, then, one thing," said Given. "Did not Emile Fleuriot overhear in the library something which made him suspect that I was not the true Vereal?"

"Most certainly, señor."

"But why under heaven, then, did he not inform the officers of the law?"

"Because, señor, he had come to love you. There is no other reason that I can see, and for his part, he will never speak of the matter. Emile Fleuriot is a man of character, as you must know, señor."

"By all means. Now for a question which you may answer or forget that I have asked it, as you will. What of my wife's mother, and of her studious father?"

Vereal studied his cigarette for a time before he replied: "They grow old, and frozen, señor. But—since you ask, I suppose I need not presume to say that I am sorry they do not send messages to their daughter?"

"They will come to that in time," said John Given. "Don Federico is like a starched collar. Time is the only water which will melt his pride. Still another question. There was the old tutor. He, I suppose, has passed away?"

"Louis Gaspard? By no means! I have built a little house for him and filled it with books. He lives there very happily and comes to see me every morning when I am breakfasting. He stands behind my chair and asks me what I am studying, and when he finds that I am only standing still, he shakes his head and sorrows for the man I might have been if I had not been a Vereal. Perhaps he is right!"

José sighed, then waved such thoughtfulness away.

"I presume that he is not much liked by the good men of San Triste?"

"On the contrary, he is adored!"

"After betraying their Vereal?"

José laughed. "That is forgotten. The people only remember that he brought me back."

When José left, Given followed him to the door.

"Come to me again," he urged. "You will always be a thousand times welcome, señor. Do not forget me."

The Vereal raised his hand and pushed back the hair along

the side of his head. A long, straight-plowed scar was revealed.

"When the wind blows in a certain way from the north," he said, "there is a tingling here which reminds me of you."

He hesitated. Then taking the hand of Given with a sudden impulse, he added: "Come to San Triste again, señor. The last gay day I had was that on which I last saw you. Come to San Triste. Tom Leven is a sad man since you have left us. Do you know what he insists on calling you? The *other* Vereal!"